Revenge of a Broken Heart

Salome B.

Copyright © 2016 Salome B.

Published by Royal-Loyalty Publications

This is a work of fiction. Any references or similarities to actual events, real people, living or dead, or to real locals are intended to give the novel a sense of reality. Any similarity in other names, characters, places, and incidents are entirely coincidental.

Salome (Lome) Bazier

salomebazier@gmail.com

Facebook: www.facebook.com/salome.bazier

Facebook Group:

https://www.facebook.com/groups/SalomeB_ReadersLounge

Dedication

I would like to dedicate my book to the memory of my cousins Johnny Gill-Ware (04/15/90-12/21/15), Runny "Jr." Gill Jr. (10/05/78-05/05/04), and my uncle their father Runny "Frog" Gill Sr. (10/27/58-09/19/95) Father and sons reunited again for all eternity. Also my twin baby girls Eri'Anna and Eri'Anashia Bebbs. Each and every one of you are truly missed; there is not a day that goes by I don't think of you love you all, gone but never forgotten. Continue to keep looking down watching over us.

Acknowledgements

I would first like to give all honor and praises to the Lord and Savior Jesus Christ and God for blessing me with this opportunity and giving me the strength to keep going even when I thought I couldn't and wouldn't make it; without you there is no me. It's true when they say what God has for you is for you, and as long as I keep my faith and focus on him, any and all things are possible. Thank you to my biggest support system and my pride and joy; my children Dasheka, Jayso'ne, and Toure', without them I don't know where I will be.

They keep me motivated and wanting to strive to accomplish my goals. Mommy loves you all with all my heart and soul, and I thank God for seeing me fit to be your parent and bringing you in my life.

To my sister, LaTanya Fry and my girl, Chanique Jones, thank you so much for pushing me and encouraging me to write and letting me know I can do anything I set my heart to do. If it wasn't for you two ladies, I never would have attempted to write this book.

To my dad, James Bazier, thank you for being the best dad you can be and for always letting me know you are there. Whether it was to pray for me or just to listen to me vent, you were always there and that means so much to me.

. My family, friends, and fans who has done nothing but supported me in all my journeys and stood by my side, I love each and every one of you guys and I can't thank you enough.

Chapter 1-Glen Park

Asha

"Damn Autumn, I can't believe you got me out here walking in 90-degree weather just to go see Dru ass!"

"Well Bitch, it ain't my fault your damn car broke down. Hell, I needed some dick, and if you were still with Loco's crazy ass you would have did the same."

We were coming from *Glen Park* and were walking down *MLK* headed to *Dorie Miller*, which is one of the many PJ's in *Gary, IN*. I was so mad at Autumn for having me in the heat walking, but I can't lie, I knew exactly where my lil cousin was coming from. See, Autumn was tall and slender standing at about 5'3; she had caramel-colored skin and hair past her shoulders. I must say my cousin was a bad Bitch; hell if I was a nigga, I would be on her. Now, me on the other hand, I'm short, bowlegged, standing at 5'1 with caramel-colored skin, hair to the middle of my back and a coke bottle body.

Me and Autumn had just moved in together; she had just graduated from *Lew Wallace High School*. Of course I have three whole years on her, but you couldn't tell when we were together. I was currently working on my second degree by attending *IU* to become an RN.

"So Asha, you just gone continue to walk in silence huh? I know damn well you can't be that mad?" says Autumn.

"Bitch shut up; it's too hot to talk!" I yelled to Autumn and we both just bust out laughing, and right on key my phone rang, "Hello?"

"Hi, is this Asha?"

"Yes,"

"Hi Asha this is Mike from *Bennies Auto*. I called to tell you that the part for your car will be in tomorrow so we should have your car up and running by tomorrow evening,"

"Okay, thank you; that is fine." I said while hanging up the phone, then Autumn chimed in.

"So wats up? Are they about to bring you your car?"

"Nope they had to order the part and it should be ready tomorrow; this just made me want to go kill Loco and his bitch ass!"

"Shit I bet; that's some bogus shit for that girl to put sugar in your tank like that. It ain't your fault Loco won't leave you along."

"Right and the killing part is I did move out and leave him along."

Right when I said that, a *Ranger Rover* drove past and we heard the dudes say, "Damn who is that? Shorty thick as hell."

Of course, me and Autumn burst out laughing because we already knew we were the shit. Me and Autumn both had on the new *Retro 8 Jay's* but she wore an all *Pink* short set from *Victoria's Secret Pink* that revealed all of her curves; her shirt made her perky size C tits peak out. I, on the other hand, had on some *Michael Kors* denim shorts with an all-white *Michael Kors* T-shirt that fitted me to the tee.

We were so deep in convo about our plans tonight and having her sister Meka come and pick us up that we never even noticed that the *Range Rover* had turned around and pulled up on the side of us.

To Autumn's surprise, the passenger was a dude by the name of Weed that she went to school wit and had a crush on; the driver on the other hand was a known drug dealer in the G; his name was Moe. Moe was beyond fine; he was light-skinned with long curly hair that he kept in braids. He had a body built like he needed to be on the cover of a magazine. His teeth were so purely white that when he smiled they sparkled. Just looking at him made my pussy wet. All the females were after Moe and down to do whatever to get a piece of him, and I wasn't down for those problems; especially after the relationship I just got out of.

"Good evening ladies; how are you", Moe said with a smile.

Weed chimed in, "Damn, I went to school with you, huh? I recognize that face anywhere."

Autumn, of course, laughed in a seductive, flirtatious way, "Yeah, you did; you were a year ahead of me I just graduated this year; never knew you even noticed me since you never said anything."

"Awe, my bad shorty. I was just on my paper and getting the hell up outta there but trust me I noticed everything about you."

"Hello Miss Lady, my name Moe. What's your name?"

"Yeah, I know who you are. I heard about you but my name Asha. Nice to meet you."

"Well, I hope they were good things, but from the sound of your voice, they weren't. You know you can't believe everything you hear Miss Asha."

Damn, just hearing him say my name did something to me. I can't lie, the nigga was fine and he knew that, and yes, I wanted him bad; so bad I could've took him right then and there, but of course, he will never know that. I'm not the type to throw myself at any man. He has to earn me. I know my worth, and I live up to it.

"Well, let's see Mr. Moe. I do believe them when they say you're the man of these streets. All the ladies want you and throw themselves at you, plus you change your women more than you change your drawers so excuse me when I say I'm not interested and

I'm not that type of female. If you would excuse me I would like to be on my way now."

As I turned to walk away, I noticed Moe was staring at me with a grin on his face like he was undressing me with his eyes, yet he has a look in his eyes like he was plotting something.

Autumn and Weed were in deep convo when I approached them, "Hey, I'm about to continue walking."

"Okay, here I come." Autumn said.

As I began my journey, I hear Moe call my name, "Hey, Miss Asha, do you mind if I give you and your girl a ride to where ever you're walking to?"

"Well, she is my cousin, and sure, we're going to *Dorie Miller*. Are you okay with that?" I asked.

"Yes ma'am; I have no problem with it. Hop in." Me and Autumn jumped in; I got in the front passenger seat, and she sat in the back with Weed. I made sure I took a mental note of Moe's ride. It was real nice… an all-black-on-black 2016 *Range Rover* with tinted windows and 22" rims; the inside had two sunroofs, 4 flat screens, and heated leather seats that were custom made.

As were riding down the street, I sat back and looked out the window in deep thought about all I just went through being with Loco. In the middle of my daydreaming, Moe interrupted me.

"Why is it a woman of your status out here walking? Where is your man at for one? Two, why he got you out here walking? You don't have a car?"

"Wow, you a lil blunt huh? And nosey, but to answer your question, I'm single; just got out of a messy relationship, and yes I have a car; it's in the shop right now."

"So what's wrong with your car and what happen between you and dude? And yes I'm being nosey; is that a problem?"

I knew exactly what Moe was up to, trying to get all the info on me he can so he can try and sweep me in, but it wasn't happening. I was hooked to his game; I'd been in this street life for too long and was too smart to let a nigga run any game on me, so I played right along like I was clueless. He gone have to try a little harder cause that might work on these other broads but not this one.

"Yes nosey is an understatement right about now. You getting personal so let's see; my car had sugar in the tank, and it's a long story about my ex that we're not about to get into next subject." Before he could get any other questions out, we were pulling up at the crib, and I was so relieved. I was shocked that he got out of the car and opened my door like a gentleman and both Weed and Moe walked us to the door. It threw me off guard when I heard Weed ask Autumn was he still going to see her tonight at *The Link Bar* considering her dude Dru was going to be there including his twin brother Dre.

Autumn and Dru been messing around for about two years now on and off, but he was her main dude. The thing is, Autumn liked to live on the wild side and explore her options as well; she says she don't want to be tied down to one dude unless he put a ring on it so she did her dirt and didn't care who liked it.

"Now girl how you gone invite that boy to the club knowing the twins are going to be there?" I asked Autumn.

"Girl stop, now you know me. All I have to do is stay on the dancefloor all night and the first one to call me once I leave will be the one to get these cookies tonight so roll this blunt up while I call Meka to see what time she coming."

"Now did you really have to start twerking in the middle of the floor like that and where the Swisher at?"

I couldn't do nothing but laugh at her little dance with no music yet she was right; she will sit there and spend the whole night on the dancefloor and not pay attention to Dru at all as if she doesn't even know him. Autumn has the mindset that, if a nigga can do it to a female, then a female can do it to a nigga and she was tired of getting played so she started playing niggas back.

Meka showed up about 15 minutes after Autumn called her with the rest of our crew Jazzy, Bonnie, Destiney, and Coco. We have all been besties since elementary and all grew up in *Glen Park* area. We always meet up at one another's house to drink, smoke, and get dressed before we stepped out. Jazzy had picked up a bottle of *Crown Royal Apple,* Destiny bought more swishers, and besides the blunt I rolled up, the others pitched in on another dime bag. We sat there chilling listening to music and talking for about two hours before actually getting ready, and out of the blue, Autumn bust out talking about me hooking up with Dre; this bitch can really ruin my high on any given day.

"So Asha, your ass know you need some dick. You need to let Dre gone and hit that and quit playing; that boy worships the ground your ass walks on." Autumn teased.

Everyone in the room just bust out into laughter; truth be told, I did have him wrapped around my little finger like a little puppy dog and never even touched the poor child.

"Naw, I'm good yall; even though he is cute and all, him and Dru are cool with Loco, and they all kick it with one another; that wouldn't be cool. This ain't keep it all in the friends' circle hell."

"Hey Autumn, I feel Asha though; they are cool with Loco, and he finds that shit out he gone try to body her ass and Dre's ass." says Meka.

"Hell I wouldn't give a fuck if it was his brother, uncle, cousin, whatever; he fucked up not Asha so his loss someone else's gain regardless of who they are why should she miss out on her night and shining armor because of who the hell Loco is cool with?" Autumn said bluntly.

"Well yea, that's true too. He could be the one you never know; hell he already trying to be there for you and do any and everything for you without you even being his girl; imagine what lengths he will do if you were his girl." says Bonnie.

And in unison everyone was in agreement, but to me, I think he was playing it dangerously. What kind of friend was he if he was willing to go behind his dude back and fuck with his girl, well ex-girl. If he can do him like that there is no telling what he would do to me if I ever got on his bad side or if things didn't work out between us if I did choose to give him a sample. While I'm in deep thought the girls all started to get dressed and ready to go out. Autumn was the first in the shower while Meka flat-ironed and curled Jazzy's hair. Destiney was putting on her makeup, Coco was oiling her body and I was still undecided on what to wear.

I ended up wearing this all-black fitted *Chanel* dress that hugged all of my curves. It had spaghetti straps, V-neckline that shows my 42 triple D cleavage, and my back was out. To top it all off, I put on my all-black red bottoms. I wore my *Pink Chiffon* body lotion and body spray from *Bath and Body Works* and my hair was down in a wrap. I must say shorty was looking good as always; We jumped into Meka's 2014 *Dodge Durango* and headed to *The Link Bar*. We were already tipsy and high as a kite, and none of us knew how we were going to stand in a line considering the line was wrapped around the building.

Upon walking to the building, we were stopped at the entrance by one of the bouncers, "Hello, excuse me Miss, Is your name Asha?"

"Who wants to know?" I snapped.

"Miss Asha, you have VIP access compliments of the owner Moe; you don't have to stand in line; let me escort you to your section."

I immediately caught a frog in my throat and looked at Autumn; Autumn looked at me. I seriously didn't know what to say; not only was this the biggest drug dealer in Gary, but he was also the owner of the club we frequent often and I had no clue.

"Well damn, Asha; this nigga really on you. Did you know this nigga owned *The Link*?" Autumn said cheesing from ear to ear.

"Um no, Autumn, I didn't; that is not something we discussed. Hell, I barely had a convo with him." As we were escorted into our section, we spotted the twins at the bar ordering drinks.

"Wait a minute bitch; is we talking about Moe, the biggest drug dealer in Gary giving you VIP access and shit when y'all hoes run into this nigga?" Meka was yelling that over the song "Ghetto" by August Alsina. I smiled and started dancing because this was my song and I sang right along with the music:

I love the way you keep them heels on

Hair ain't yours but it's paid for and it's real long

Show them tattoos when you switch it up

With your J's on

As I was dancing, Moe walks up on me and started dancing with me from behind, and of course, I had to show him I wasn't to be played with when it came down to dancing. All the girls stood shocked watching me twerk on him like we were having sex in the middle of our VIP section. We really put on a show, and of course, all the other females in the club peeped it out and was jealous. For the remainder of the night, I received all kinds of hateful stares. If looks can kill, I was a dead motherfucker.

Moe took our drink orders and said it was on the house. I ordered a top shelf *Long Island Ice Tea*; the rest of the crew got a bottle of *Henny*. Autumn peeped Weed coming towards us and Dru was eyeing her every move so she immediately grabbed me and Meka to head to the dancefloor; the rest of the crew followed.

We stayed on the dance floor the rest of the night, Autumn eventually danced with Dru and Weed with no complications. Of course Dru knew the deal when Autumn went out and got on the dance floor. He never tripped on other dudes dancing with her. He wasn't the jealous type. Meka ended up being booed up with her baby Mike, Jazzy was getting hit on by some random dude, Coco's baby dad was there and took her off to a corner somewhere doing God knows what. Me, Bonnie, and Destiney were on the floor clowning and singing Nikki Minaj's song "High School":

He said he came from Jamaica, he owned a couple acres

A couple fake visas cause he never got his papers

Gave up on love fucking with them heart breakers

But he was getting money with the movers and the shakers

Of course random niggas were trying to grind on us, and out of nowhere, Dre comes and grabs me when they played the throwback Janet Jackson "Would You Mind":

Cause I'm gonna

Bathe you, play with you, rub you, caress you

Tell you how much I've missed you

I just wanna

Why the hell they play this song, I have no clue, but the way that boy picked me up and held me on that wall and danced with me like he was a stripper, I swear I had an orgasm like five times. Damn. If I didn't want him then, I sure in the hell want him now. If his dick game was as good as he danced, he can get all my cookies. Or maybe that was the liquor and weed talking because I was horny as fuck after that.

Once the song was over, Dre went back over to the bar where his brother was and I see the girls looking at me smiling and shaking their head so I walk back over to the VIP section to join them.

"Well, what do we have here? Did Dre just put it on Asha or did he put it on her? Girl, you betta hit that. Hell looking at y'all just made my pussy wet, so I know yours is wet as hell!!!" says Jazzy while we all just laughed.

The night was ending, and I went well beyond my limit of drinks because I was drunk off my ass but was still aware of my surroundings. Coco ended up leaving with her baby daddy and the rest of us were back on the dance floor. "No Love" by Lil Scrappy played then the club got turnt up when Future "Move That Dope" played. All you heard throughout the club was

Young nigga move that dope

Young nigga move that dope

They move that dope, they move that dope

Young nigga move that dope

You would have thought our feet would have been hurting from all the dancing we did but we live that DIVA life status; we do this for a living. We all loved to wear heels and dance. It was close to closing time and the DJ was playing the last four songs, and we stayed on the floor the whole time. K-Camp "Blessing" played, and what do you know, here comes Moe grinding on me to this song and singing it in my ear telling me I'm a blessing:

> Want you to know you're a
>
> Blessing
>
> Yeah baby girl you're a
>
> Blessing

Of course, I couldn't help but to blush; he was really trying to get me to fall for him, and truth be told, it was really working. He was smooth, but little did he know that it wasn't going to be that easy. Surprisingly, Moe stayed on the dance floor with me and even danced with me to Bryson Tiller "Don't":

> Don't play with her don't be dishonest
>
> Still not understanding this logic
>
> Aye, I'm back and I'm better

I want you bad as ever

We were getting it to this song. It seemed like it was just me and him and anyone and everything around us just disappeared. Nothing else mattered; just us. I think the DJ got a whiff of our vibe because he had the nerve to play my favorite song "Treat Me Like Somebody" by Tink, which of course I had to sing it to Moe since he sung to me:

I just want somebody

To treat me like somebody

Won't be like everybody

All you gotta do is love me for me baby.

Lastly, they played Wale "The Body"

Baby you got a body like a Benz

And I'm just tryna drive it once again

And that's what we ended our club night on. Of course me and Moe had another show going on in the middle of the dance floor, and I left him standing there with a straight hard-on, which I felt through his pants.

We all got into Meka's ride to go home. On the radio, they were playing Rich Homie Quan "Walk Thru". Of course they wouldn't let the whole scene of me and Moe go. I had informed them about our encounter walking with Autumn to get some dick from Dru earlier that day, and right on cue, Dru called Autumn to tell her that he will meet her at our house. He wanted to know if he could bring Dre. As soon as I was about to say yes, 'cause honestly, after that dance I really wanted to know what that dick do, we pulled up to our house, and Loco's ass was sitting on my porch. All types of hell was about to hit the fan now.

"Um Dru, I don't think it's a good idea for you to bring Dre right now cuz Loco sitting on the porch waiting on Asha and it is 3 am." Autumn said with concern.

"Okay, I'm on my way. Hope this nigga ain't about to act stupid before I get there." Dru replied.

"Okay." Autumn ended the call, and we both walked up to the front door.

"What are you doing here Loco? It's 3 am; you have no business at my damn house." I snapped.

He not even knowing I already put a bullet in the chamber before I stepped foot out the car; shit was about to get real tonight.

Chapter 2-Escape

Asha

"Asha I just want to talk to you; I didn't come over here on some bullshit. I just want to have a face to face convo, that's all. Can you please give me that?" Loco pleaded.

"Really Loco? You should've thought about that before the bitch you fucked in our house put sugar in my damn tank. Better yet, you should have talked to me before you brought another bitch in the crib."

"You right, and I'm not here to point the finger or argue. Can we please talk like adults, and here, this is for your car, and I'm really sorry about that."

Right then and there, he gave me six stacks for my car which was way more than what it cost to get it fixed, but hey, I wasn't going to complain. He should of gave me that after what he put me through. As soon as he handed me the money, Dru walks up, "What's up Loco and Asha? Everything cool?"

"Hey Dru. Yea, we cool. Autumn in the house waiting on you." I responded back to Dru.

Dru looked at Loco like he was crazy trying to make sure he wasn't on no shit. "Loco, you cool dog?"

"Yea Dru. I ain't on shit. Just trying to talk to Asha that's all."

"Alright y'all. Let me go in here with my lady; I'll holler at y'all." Dru said before walking away.

I turned and looked at Loco and told him let's go talk; we went up to my room. I knew that talking to him was a big mistake because that is how he always sucked me back into his good graces. It was just something about his caramel-colored skin, hazel brown eyes, 6'1 built body, and the way he looked at me that I loved so much. Not to mention, his sex game was on point, and I loved all 12-inches of his long, thick, and juicy dick. Me and Loco were each other's middle school sweethearts. I mean, from the 6th grade till recently, and we both were now 21 years old. We had that love/hate relationship where one minute we fought like niggas on the street who didn't know one another, then the next minute, we were Romeo and Juliet.

I noticed Loco was looking at me with that "I'm about to tear that pussy up" look in his eyes and licking his lips. Needless to say, I was already drunk and horny as hell, so he was definitely getting the cookies tonight.

"Damn Asha, you looking really good tonight. Did you have fun?"

I smirked at his comment, put Bryson Tiller's CD on, and started to grind to the song *"Exchange"*.

"Well you said you wanted to talk so talk."

Truth be told I wasn't near bout trying to hear what he had to say. We were done for good this time, but anytime I wanted the dick, I knew I could get it with no problems; it was still mine   no matter what.

Right then and there, he pushed me up against the wall and started tongue kissing me down none stop. I wasn't trying to push him away. We got to tearing each other's clothes off and going to town with each other's tongues. Out of nowhere, this nigga picked me up to where I can literally touch the ceiling. He had me propped up against the wall, ripped my panties off, and pushed his tongue deep inside of my pussy moving it in and out and around in a circle while his index figure played with my clit. My eyes instantly rolled in the back of my head as he fucked me with his tongue. I can't lie, this nigga's head game was lyfe; he didn't lack in those skills at all. He made sure I came at least six times from his head game along.

He laid me gently on the bed and put all 12" in me. He made sure to go in deep to make me gasp and grip his arms. He smirked and raised my legs up over my head and held them there as he pounded the shit out of my pussy. Even though I was drunk I knew what I was doing. Little did Loco know this was the goodbye sex. I had to get it one more time before I actually walked completely away. This was going to be one of the hardest tasks I would do to walk away from someone I truly love and had my heart. I been dealing with him for over 10 years but it had to end.

See Loco wasn't just crazy in the streets; he was also a woman beater, and technically, I was too fine to keep fighting this nigga on a regular basis. It got so bad till I literally had to up strap on him; that's when I knew it had to end right then and there. One of us was going to end up dead and I be damned if it was me. I have to admit this is not the first time I tried to walk away. Somehow I always went back to him but this time it went too far. Out of all the shit me and Loco been through, I never thought he would disrespect me to this extent to bring another woman in my home and in our bed. There is no coming back from this no matter how hard he tried.

See me and Loco had a nice ass crib out there in Merrillville, IN which is only like five minutes from Gary. Loco may not be the biggest drug dealer in Gary but he is a hustler and keep his money stacked so we were never hurting. He has always been the type of nigga to wine and dine me all through school; he kept me with the best shit. Don't get me wrong, I never needed a nigga to take care of me. My bank account always stayed above 10 stacks, plus I'm my father's only child so I'm very spoiled and daddy made sure his baby girl was well taken care of no matter what. Once I graduated from *Lew Wallace* my dad made sure I was set for life.

So the big question is how did I end up in the PJ's in Gary, IN. Well, once I graduated from high school, I got a job at *Methodist Hospital Northlake* as a PCA. I was making good money to be only 18 years old at the time, and truthfully, I didn't have to work, but living in the G, you have to keep a low profile. I never wanted anyone to know what my bank account looked like. Gary is big on haters and people not only wanted to kill you for living on the wrong side of Broadway, but they will kill you just because you got something they don't have. And working only made my bank account bigger than what it was. Not to mention Loco was adding to it as well.

Our house was a nice three-bedroom home with two full sized bathrooms and a half bathroom downstairs. Our basement was a fully finished basement; the house was completely furnished from top to bottom, and the two car garage housed my 2016 *GMC* fully loaded *Acadia* along with Loco 2015 *Escalade*. In the driveway, I kept my 2014 *Volkswagen Jetta*; this was my low-key profile car. Now, I'm going to remember this day like it was yesterday. I ended up applying for *Gary Housing Authority* during one of me and Loco's fights and he ended up blacking my eye; in return, I sat his car on fire. He had an old school *Chevy Impala.* The year, I believe, was 1961, and he had it looking sweet. Besides me, that was his other baby. That bitch was sitting on some twenty-two's, chromed out rims, and it was painted candy apple red; had the whole passenger side dashboard taken out and made into a big, flat screen TV.

It had at least six speakers and the interior was custom made white leather with the red embroidery lettering that had his name and mines in the seats. Yea, I straight torched that shit when he blacked my eye... poured gasoline all over and whoosh there it went. And I took pics of it and sent it to him while it was on fire.

At that time, I went back to my dad's house and applied for housing even though I could afford a crib. I wanted to be somewhere I knew he wouldn't come too often. Plus, he was on the no trespass list. This was my little escape plan. Eventually, I ended up going back home to him but I knew deep down inside it wasn't for long.

Thing is, our landlord was sweet on me so all I had to do was tell

him my plan to leave Loco and give him my number to call me when

I left and he will take me off the lease with no consequences. But

going back home to him after he begged and begged for days some

things didn't seem right.

Everyone said I shouldn't trust him after I torched his car;

that was grounds for him to kill me knowing how much he loved that

car and how much money he put in it, but trust and believe, I stayed

with my piece on me. My dad made sure of that. See my dad was in

the navy and I get my knowledge of guns from him so I didn't fuck

with those purse guns like 22 calibers like normal females. I had a 9

mm *Smith and Wesson;* it was black and chrome with two 17 round

clips, and I kept them both with me and fully loaded with 35 bullets,

one in the chamber and both clips full with 17 rounds. I didn't play

no games, so I was more than confident to go home. I didn't win the

championship on the rifle team for nothing so my aim was sweet.

I was always taught that a woman's intuition is never wrong. Something with Loco this time around was not right. Mind you, we have been down this road plenty of times. Break up and make up… even through his cheating tactics, we got over it but this time I couldn't put my finger on it. I kept hearing talk around town that he was fucking with this stripper chick named Cinnamon and she had his head gone. He was tricking off on her like it was no tomorrow and like he didn't have a girl and she was his main chick. Loco never been the one to stay out too late or stay out all night, but this seemed to be one of his brand new habits. Funny this happened as soon as he had proposed to me when he begged me to come back to him.

I worked the midnight shift and more and more as I came home I noticed things out of place, jewelry lying around the house, and my house smelling like cheap perfume. I just knew this nigga did not have the balls to bring a hoe in our house. As many times as he called himself stepping out throughout the years, he never stooped this low; this was all brand new to me. When asked what was going on and whose belongings they were, he will give me a lame ass excuse that

Jay and one of his chicken-heads came over and kicked it with him.

So I put my plan in place to catch Loco up in his lie. If this nigga had a girl in my crib and bed he will be lucky to make it out of this alive.

"Hey Autumn, I need to talk to you. Are you busy?"

"No, what's wrong Asha? Everything okay?"

"I will explain everything when I get there. Call the girls and have them meet me at your house, is Meka there?"

"Yes she is here and I will get the girls in route."

I headed over to my Auntie Tammy's house to tell the girls my plan on catching Loco up. I told them what I was feeling and the little things I was finding around the house. I wanted Autumn to move in with me since she had graduated already and was already looking for her own house. Meka and Mike lived together already; I knew moving out for good will cause hell with Loco's ass so it had to be done on the low regardless of what happened because I never fully packed all my shit and just left. Autumn called the twins and told them what the deal was and informed them that I needed help moving, Meka called Mike, and CoCo called her baby daddy Sean.

They all knew that I was planning to act like I had to work but really didn't so I can sneak up on him and the girl in my house. On November 20th, it went down; I got up and got dressed for work like any other work day. Loco was downstairs smoking a blunt and playing the game as usual. I yelled down the stairs and told him I was leaving so he came up and gave me a hug and kiss goodbye. I drove to Jazzy's house and put my car in her garage, and we jumped in the rental Jazzy got just for tonight and drove back to my house. We parked down the street so I can see who comes and goes from my house, and right when we pulled up and shut down the engine and lights not even three minutes after that Loco come running out the house and jumps in his truck.

"So Jazzy where you think he going at 1 am?" Jazzy just looked at me and shook her head. My phone rang with Autumn, Bonnie, Destiney, and CoCo all on the line.

"So what's going on?" the girls all said in union.

"He just pulled off in his truck."

"Well damn. Where he going at this hour?" Meka yelled in the background cuz Autumn had the phone on speaker.

"Your guess is as good as mines, and if he pulls up with a chick, I'm going to jail." I said confidently.

Thirty minutes later, here he comes with this bitch Cinnamon and immediately Jazzy says, "OH MY GOD, HE DIDN'T!!!" She instantly picked up the phone and called the girls back to cue them in. I was so furious I felt my blood boiling and my eyes were red as fuck. I grabbed my gun from under the seat and reached for the door handle. Jazzy grabbed me just in time, "Asha wait a minute; you have to be smart about this and actually catch him in the act; don't just run up in there like GI Jane bitch and put that damn gun down. No one is going to jail tonight. You know what you have to do after this, now we can beat her ass but we ain't killing anyone."

Deep down, I knew Jazzy was right, but my anger was trying to take over so I gave her a look that could have burned a hole through her heart.

"Bitch I don't care about you looking at me like that; you know I'm right."

"Yeah you're right. I'm not going to kill the bitches but I just might pistol whip one of them."

We sat and waited for about 30 minutes before going in and I ran full speed to my bedroom. As soon as we entered the house, we knew off top he was deep in her nasty ass pussy cuz all we heard is her moaning and screaming before we even stepped foot in the house. I kicked in the door, and he jumped up like he seen a ghost. Before I knew it, I had pulled the trigger. The bullet missed his head only by a few inches; if he wouldn't have never moved his head he was a goner.

Jazzy yelled, "Asha no," and snatched the gun from me. This bitch Cinnamon had the nerve to be screaming like she didn't know this was my shit. This bitch knew all about me and she had the balls not only to fuck with my man but to do it at my house. The thought of that pissed me off even more and I charged dead for her.

I heard Loco in the background yelling, "Asha, baby stop; calm down, Asha. I'm sorry!"

I have no clue what happened next because I blacked out and all I seen was blood everywhere and Jazzy yelling, "Asha stop, you're going to kill her; she losing consciousness."

Then Loco had the nerve to grab me and stop me from pounding this bitch head on the ground. Now why he did that I have no clue; that made me madder. I looked at him, ran to the kitchen, and got a knife, and came charging after him.

"Asha quit fucking playing; put the knife down Asha!" he says as he running towards the door. Jazzy then steps in front of the door and says, "Asha, you can't do this. Someone is going to call the police; you know what it is so let's just leave; you have your plan in place."

With that being said, we left and all meet up at my hotel room. I have no clue what happened to Cinnamon… if she went to the hospital, called the police, or what. At this point, I didn't care. I was too hurt. That whole night, Loco blew my phone up to the point I added him on the block list so he started having his sister call me. Autumn took my phone and turned it off and all the girls stayed the night with me. The boys had the keys to the house so they can go and pack up my things and take it to the new house in the PJ's. Word is Loco was scared to go back to the house so he stayed at Jay's crib for a few days.

Loco finally came back home three days later thinking I had calmed down not knowing I moved out. He walked into the house and the only thing that was there was the furniture he owned and his clothes along with the bed he fucked his bitch in. I laid the keys on the kitchen counter with my engagement ring. Cinnamon was so pissed that I beat the shit out of her she came to my job and put two bags of sugar in my tank and bragged about it. It took about three weeks before I actually seen Loco again; he had been everywhere looking for me. He never knew I had a crib in Dorie Miller; that was the last place he would look so I knew it was the perfect escape route. Till the night he ended up on my doorstep, the last time I seen him I ran him down with my car and actually pinned him between my car and the yellow poles that the pay phones sit in between. I pulled off not knowing if I killed him or if he was okay. Well considering we just had sex, and he's lying in my bed, I guess he doing just fine.

Chapter 3-Crawl Back

Loco

Man, I really fucked up this time with Asha, but I couldn't lose her to no pussy ass niggas out here. I have to do any and everything to get her back, and I'm on a mission to do just that. Me and Asha been fucking around with one another since the sixth grade and she has been my ride or die since. Yea, I admit I done dipped and dabbed here and there with other females, but it never came down to this between me and Asha. Messing around with Cinnamon just turned the tables on my ass completely. Then again, I also never been so bold to bring a hoe to the crib either, but after Asha torched my car, I just didn't give a fuck. Now, I'm paying for it.

See I was so fucked up when Asha torched my shit; I got drunk and high as a kite and went out to the strip joint in Chicago called *The Factory* right off of S. Doty Ave. This is of course where Cinnamon works at, yet she from the hood so I already knew her. I'd just never fucked with shorty like that. I knew Cinnamon had a crush on me from back in the day, but she never acted on it till this one particular night I showed up at the club. I thought it was kind of strange because she knew about Asha. Hell, we all went to school together, and Asha wasn't a secret. Yet me being so fucked up, and I was still drinking and smoking weed along with popping that Molly, I went right along with shorty's seduction.

Since I frequent this club a lot, I have my very own VIP room that I get every time I'm here. It just so happens that Cinnamon was the one who was giving me my private show. If I didn't know any better, I would say shorty set that shit up as soon as she seen me walk through the door, because she has never given me a private show. Shorty came in and immediately got to working that pole to Wale's song, "Bad". All I knew is shorty was bad as hell that night, but right on cue as I'm bobbing my head when I hear:

Is it bad that I never made love, no I never did it

But I sure know how to fuck I'll be your

Bad girl, I'll prove it to you

Cinnamon just whipped a nigga dick out from nowhere and sucked the shit out of my shit like it was no tomorrow. I felt all my kids leave that night. Baby girl even swallowed every last drop; I was mesmerized. Now I know the weed, liquor, and Molly had something to do with it, but I had to have shorty right then and there. A nigga dick was on swole, and she knew it. Shorty laid back and spread her legs like a bald eagle on takeoff. All I seen was her pretty little pink pussy all in my face and she laid there flicking and playing with her clit back and forth with her index finger and made those pretty little moaning noise while she did it.

As soon as I straddled her ready to enter, she took that same finger she played with her clit with and sucked on it while I entered her precious little pussy, and it gripped my dick so hard and pulled me all the way in. I felt like I was in heaven. Cinnamon being a stripper did her some justice cuz all the little tricks she was doing on a nigga dick had a nigga going crazy. I was loving every bit of it. The way we were fucking you would have thought we were filming a porno; shorty was calling me daddy, and the louder she got, the harder and deeper I went pounding the shit out of her pussy like it was the last thing on this earth Shorty even took all 12' in the ass like it wasn't nothing. This was the first for me because me and Asha don't do anal sex so from that point on I hated to admit it, but shorty had me hooked, and from the looks in her eyes, she knew it. That was the beginning of a disaster waiting to happen and I fell right for it all.

Now don't get me wrong, shorty will never amount to what me and Asha have and she can never be Asha, but she did take me away from the anger I felt towards Asha for burning my ride up. Not to mention I will never actually leave Asha for another woman, yet I am a man, and it's hard to turn down some pussy. Especially the way Cinnamon put it on me. Thinking about how I got my dumb ass into this shit and knowing that I was about to lose the love of my life for good over some pussy had me bugging. I wasn't leaving Asha even if my life depended on it; a nigga was going to have to take me out before I let them take my spot in Asha's life. Thinking about all that made me turn over, and grab Asha, and hold her tight. I prayed she gave me another chance after she listened to what I had to say since I did come over here to talk, yet talking never happened which I think was a good thing.

Walking into the house after Asha caught me with Cinnamon damn near killed my ass when I saw that all her shit was moved out. That shit hurt me like hell; I wouldn't wish that kind of pain on my worst enemy for real, for real. Right then and there, I went searching for her to see where she was. My first stop was to her dad's house, and he instantly upped a chopper on me soon as he seen me at the door. I can't blame him though; I was the last person he wants his one and only child/princess to be with after all we been through. I figured Asha wouldn't go there since she knew that was the first place I would go looking but I had to check. After about a month, I caught up with her on 35th and Broadway at the Dairy Queen and she hit me with her car for even approaching her. She still wasn't over the shit yet; I still wasn't ready to give up; our love was stronger than that.

Asha was cool with my sister Netta, and they had stayed in touch regardless of what we been through; they stayed tight and had an unbreakable bond as well. Netta instantly got on me when she heard what went down and told me I deserve to lose her. In actuality, she was right but I wasn't trying to hear that shit. Since Netta and Asha kept in touch, I was able to get her address and whereabouts from my sis. Netta knew Asha didn't want me to know where she lived and Asha also figured since I wasn't allowed in none of Gary PJs, I wouldn't dare step foot on those grounds. She thought wrong though Netta didn't have a problem with giving me her address cuz at the end of the day, she was my sister and she was going to ride for her brother regardless. I was stepping foot anywhere to go claim what was mine regardless of the circumstances.

As soon as I got the address, I headed straight there. I was sure, by it being a weekend, Asha was out with her girls as usual and I was right, but I was prepared to wait. I arrived at *Dorie Miller* around 11:30 pm. Asha did not make it back till around 3 am so yea a nigga was determined to sit outside and wait three and a half hours but it needed to be done. I had to get her back by any means necessary and come clean with it all. I can tell by the look on Asha and Autumn's face that I was the last person they expected to see on their doorstep. I knew Asha like the back of my hand so I'm sure she thought I was there on some bullshit; she cocked her gun back before she even got out the car. I didn't care about none of that though; I just wanted my baby back. Not to mention she was looking fine as hell as she always does except tonight she was mesmerizing and I wasn't even high or drunk; I was sober than a bitch.

Once I sat my eyes on her, my little man rose to attention, and I had to have her but I also had to keep my cool to get my point across. I was on a mission. I can tell Asha was drunk on her ass so we weren't going to get much talking done and me being inside her sweet, wet, juicy pussy was home. Regardless of how many times I stepped out on her, I knew where home was. Asha was always horny as hell when she was drunk so the minute we got to her room I was rock hard, but this wasn't just no fucking situation this time. I wanted to please her every way possible and show her how much I loved and cared about her. I made love to Asha like I never had before, ate her pussy like it was my last meal, and sucked every last drop of cum she had to give me out that sweet sexy pussy of hers. She had like six orgasms along just by me eating her out. Her pussy was so wet I had to control myself from busting a nut quick as hell but I wasn't trying to hold out either.

Altogether, Asha had nine orgasms which is more than she ever had in one night since we been together. I came inside her freely five times not pulling out at all, and we were mostly really careful about these type of things. Neither one of us were ready for kids but at this point I was willing to impregnate her, wife her, whatever it took. I can honestly say her sperm count should have been higher than mines as much as I filled her up. While I was in deep thought about what had occurred, Asha had awoken and immediately looked at me and said I needed to leave. I was shocked that she even said that considering the night we had and we still haven't had our conversation about us yet.

"Asha we need to talk; that was the purpose of me coming over here remember. At least give me the chance to plead my case before you put a nigga out; just hear me out."

"For what Loco? What's the point? It is what it is. You showed me how much love and respect you have for me when you brought another woman in our bed."

"Asha I'm sorry. I fucked up, I know this, but I do love you and want to be with you. I was only fucking with that girl out of anger for you burning up my car. Now, I know that is no excuse, but that's how it happened. I had no intention on things spiraling the way they did."

"Yea, you're right. That's no excuse, and I'm not buying it considering the fact that happen like four months ago. Besides, this is not what I want. I'm tired of you cheating on me and disrespecting me. I know what I'm worth, and I deserve so much better than what you have to offer me. Plus, that lets me know you been messing around with her for four months so I'm sure it's more to it than what you say."

"I'm no longer messing with her and I haven't heard from her or seen her since that night, and after last night, how can you sit here and just be so nonchalant about the situation. You actually mean to tell me it's just that easy for you to walk away from me with all the history we got. Where is your love at in the situation?"

As soon as I said that Asha got up out the bed and got dressed while throwing me my clothes at the same time. She looked at me while opening her bedroom door and stated, "See Loco, that's the thing. We have too much history of the same shit over and over again. It's a cycle with you, and I feel like I'm on a merry-go-round that I need off of, so once again, I need you to leave."

"So just like that, out of all this time we're really done? You're just giving up on us just like that? Yet you say you love me though. You don't just walk away from love Asha; you fight for it. I told you I cut the girl off completely, so why you still trippin?"

"You have to be kidding me! This is why I'm walking away. You feel it's okay to do the things you do; and I'm just supposed to accept it and take you back all the time. No that's not happening! A nigga will only do what you allow them to do. I'm done allowing you to fuck me over and steady put your hands on me like I'm not shit! Yes, I love you with all my heart, and because of that I'm going to love you enough to walk away and let you go. Cause at the end of the day, I love myself too."

"So what was last night to you Asha?"

"Goodbye sex nigga so see ya and I wish you the best."

Her telling me that made me want to wrap my hands around her neck and choke the shit out of her but I held my composure. I politely told her I wasn't giving up and I would fight for her for as long as it took and that I loved her. I also made it clear to her that I be damn if another nigga takes my place. He will have to kill me before he can have her. As soon as I said that, I got a text from Cinnamon. She had been calling since that night and I've been avoiding her last convo we had. I let her know I was done, and I wanted to be with Asha. But this text just blew my mind when I read it. Cinnamon has been calling and trying to tell me she was pregnant with my baby. Now what the hell am I going to do? Asha find this shit out she really never coming back and I can't have that. On top

of that, when she opens the front door, this nigga Moe standing at

the door, *What The Fuck Is This Shit!!!*

Chapter 4-The Wake-up Call

Asha

I had so much going through my mind I didn't know what to do. Looking at Moe and Loco standing in the doorway staring at each other like they were about to kill one another had me spooked. Not to mention the reason why Moe was at my house to begin with, who the hell was texting Loco to make him look like he had just seen a ghost after reading the text, plus the occurrence that happened between me and Loco last night. I was a ticking time bomb ready to explode right then and there; I was stressed and didn't know how to cope with things. I finally broke the awkward silence and asked Moe what was he doing at my house and told Loco bye. Moe just smiled and held up a set of car keys and said, "Here is your car Miss Lady," dropped them in my hand, and walked away.

I was speechless because first off, how did Moe know where my car was and what type of car I had? Loco laughed and said, "So is that why you so willing to walk away?" I shook my head no but at the same time I closed the door in Loco face. Once I turned around, I see Autumn standing there with her mouth open.

"Damn Asha what the fuck just happen girl?"

We both laughed and all I can say was, "I don't even know but it looks like Moe just paid for my car to get fixed and dropped it off to me in front of Loco which really don't matter because I let Loco completely go last night."

"For real girl, are you serious because from what I heard last night, it doesn't seem like you let that nigga go. Hell, y'all was getting it in big time. I thought me and Dru was doing the damn thing. Yall outdid us shit."

"Girl that was goodbye sex so I had to upstage yall and where Dru at anyway?" We both laughed at the same time.

"He still upstairs sleep but what are you about to do? Get ready for class?"

"Yes ma'am, I will talk to you later."

I headed back up the stairs to shower and get ready for class. While in the shower, I constantly kept thinking what will make Moe pick up my car without my permission and why will they let him not

knowing the status between me and him. What if he was my stalker

or something? The sad part is I don't even have Moe number to even

ask what the meaning of all this was. Hell, I just met you 48 hours

ago. Plus, I was also hurt and sad about me and Loco's situation. I

mean, this man has my whole heart and has been my soul partner

since the 6th grade. Even though I know this is what's best I'm not

nearly happy that it came to this. Thinking about this I instantly

broke down in the shower. I haven't cried about what went on when

I caught him in our home and now everything just seems to come

out and I couldn't control. It felt as if I was having a nervous

breakdown and I had to get myself together and fast because I had a

whole nursing exam today so I needed a clear head.

Once I gained my composure, I got dressed in my all white

nursing scrubs, with my all white *Air Force One's* and had my hair

in a wrap. I grabbed my book bag and headed out the door grabbing

a banana and an orange to put on my stomach with a glass of OJ. I

have to admit it felt good to drive myself to school and once I noticed that Moe left a single rose in the passenger seat with a note that said, "I shouldn't have to see you walking anymore. Enjoy having your car back Moe," with his phone number on it. I made a mental note of his number and smiled, laid it back on the passenger seat, and proceeded to class. I was happy as hell that I only worked three days a week and went to school three days a week, and I didn't have to work tonight, so that gave me some me time to myself when I got out of here. I went to school Monday and Wednesday, and Thursday was my clinical day from 7 am-3 pm. The rest of class was 9 am-2. I only worked on Tuesday, Friday, and Saturday morning 12-hour shift 6 am-6 pm.

I loved my schedule because it still gave me enough time to myself plus kick it with the ladies and study in between. I was an honor student rocking with a 3.8 GPA and there was nothing or no one that I will allow to stand in the way of my dreams and goals regardless of what I was going through. As class ended and I got in my car, my phone started ringing. Of course it had to be Netta which I'm guessing Loco must of vented to her already so she calling to be nosy. I instantly answered with an attitude because I know she the reason he knew my whereabouts anyway. All she can do was say, "Girl, you know that's my brother, and I'm team y'all any day so you really walking away this time or are you just saying this out of anger?"

"Yes, I can admit I was still angry as hell but it was truly over this time. I am really ending a 10+ year relationship just like that," I explained to Netta.

Even though she didn't blame me and said we have been through a lot over the years, at the end of the day, I had to do what is best for me, regardless of if I was with her brother or not. She still got much love and respect for me, and we will always be cool; she will always be there. I ended the call with Netta and instantly called Moe, "Hello!"

"Hello can I speak to Moe?"

"Hello Miss Lady; I see you got my note I left for you. How is the car driving?"

I let out a little smirk, "It's fine, thank you. May I ask what made you do that and how did you even know where my car was?"

"Miss Lady, I make it my business to know everything I need to know in something or someone that catches my interest, next question?"

"Well, how is it that they were just so willy-nilly to give you my car and keys not knowing if I really knew you and how much do I owe you?"

"I got my connections, and that's an insult to ask what you owe me. I didn't ask you for anything. You can pay me by not walking in these Gary streets again. That's good enough for me." And just like that, he ended the call with nothing else said, so now basically I'm speechless; this nigga really trying to win me over I see.

After me and Moe's call ended, I proceeded home in deep thought. All I could think about was my life with Loco, everything I went through with him, and how hard I fought for the love I thought we had. I just couldn't understand how he could betray me like that yet sit in my face and say he loved me. What have I ever done to deserve this type of treatment? It was one thing to me that he was even cheating, but to bring that shit and put it in my face and in my home was something I just couldn't shake. I never really had the time to sit down and think about what happened; I just went on about my business like it was nothing, but deep down inside, I was truly hurt. This whole situation took me to another level and tore me apart. I was becoming depressed and really needed some time to myself. I guess seeing Loco and having sex with him last night really brought my feelings out.

Once I made it home, I was glad the house was empty. I immediately went to my room and got in my PJs. I made sure to put my phone on "Do Not Disturb" so I wouldn't be bothered. I really needed to be to myself. I didn't have homework which was a good thing. I can take all the time I needed to reflect on everything that has occurred. I turned on the radio and laid down in the bed. The first song that came on was Ciara "I Bet". I have no clue why I even bothered to sing along with the radio because once I did that, all hell

broke loose once I said:

I bet you start loving me

Soon as I start loving someone else

Somebody better than you

I bet you start needing me

It seems as if with every lyric I sang, I cried harder and

screamed louder. I trashed my room so bad it looked like Hurricane

Katrina had come and went through this motherfucker. The last thing

I remembered was ripping up every single picture I had of me and

Loco together and everything else was a blur. I woke up to Dre

giving me a plate of food. As I looked around, I saw Autumn and

Dru in the doorway just standing there.

Autumn had a scared look on her face and then she said, "Can

I please talk to her along?" The twins left out immediately and

Autumn sat next to me on the bed. "Asha are you okay? What is going on? You had us scared shitless?" So now, I'm speechless and lost because I have no idea what Autumn is referring to. I look into the mirror and noticed my eyes were red, puffy, and swollen. I also had tears stained down my face, a headache outta of this world, and my room was trashed.

"Damn, what time is it? How long was I asleep?"

"Girl I don't know how long you were sleep but we blew your phone up."

I looked at my phone and it was 3 am. I literally been sleep for 12 hours.

"Asha what happen to your room?"

"My bad girl; I had a meltdown thinking about Loco and I trashed the room and passed out doing it. Hell I got 20 missed calls and 12 text messages."

"Well, I'm sure some of those calls are from us. We couldn't get a hold of you so we had Dre come check on you. He ended up calling us back and said you were sleep and described the situation so he stayed and cooked dinner for you."

"Awe that was nice of him and it's pretty good too." We both laughed at the same time and I have to admit that that was the first time I laughed so hard in a while.

"Asha Dre really cares for you. What if he is really the one?"

"I don't know Autumn; he is cool with Loco, and I'm not ready to deal with another dude for that matter."

"I feel you though girl. Come on, let's clean your room." We both got up and tended to my mess and instantly the twins walked back in to help. Everyone was so concerned about me but understood the circumstances and gave me my space which I really appreciated. I kept my phone on "Do not disturb" and decided to return everyone else's calls later.

Once we were done, I thanked Dre for making me dinner. I really didn't know that the boy had skills in the kitchen like that to make a home cooked meal. Autumn and Dru left out and went to her room. Dre sat and talked to me and we ended up laying down and cuddling in my bed watching TV. I was so shocked and surprised because he was a true gentleman; he didn't try to touch me or make no kind of moves on me. He just laid with me the whole time. He was so concerned about my well-being and making sure I was comfortable and our convo was like no other. I gained more respect for him because he treated me like a queen.

Waking up in Dre's arms felt so good and so right. Honestly, I was scared of that feeling and just wanted to run the other way. "Good morning beautiful, are you hungry? Would you like breakfast?"

Wow, so now he is making me breakfast in bed? This is too good to be true, and I'm not even with this man, gosh.

"Yes, thank you," Dre instantly got up, kissed me on the cheek, and left the room. Out of nowhere, I turn back over in bed then I hear Autumn and Dru going at it again this early in the morning. Them two just don't stop, so I got my headphones and listened to Pandora on my phone till Dre brought my plate of food. After we all ate and got dressed, the twins proceeded to go home so me and Autumn can do what we needed to do before I had to go to work and boy I tell you, as soon as we walked outside, here comes

Loco yelling, "For real Asha? This what you on so you just gone sit

here and start fucking around with my nigga like that, and bitch you

gone go behind my back and fuck my girl?" and then Loco just pulls

a gun out on Dre.

Chapter 5-The Setup

Cinnamon

I don't know who the fuck Loco think he is to just try and walk away from me like that and ignore my phone calls. Hell he got the wrong bitch. Once I got you and you got a taste of this pussy nigga, you were mines and I will do any and everything to prove that. On top of that, he actually thought I was gone sit here and let him go back to Asha's ass without shit happening after she jumped on me. Then to top it off I had to find out I was 14 weeks pregnant while in the hospital after the occurrence. Yea this nigga and this bitch got another thang coming. You can't get rid of CINNAMON ass just like that.

Now me and Loco have been fucking around for about four months since I threw this pussy on him at the club I strip at and hooked the nigga right around my pinky finger. Now I know some people might feel a certain way and think I'm a thot for coming after another woman man but hell that bitch had it coming after how she did me. See I been knowing them since middle school and even though me and Asha was never tight like that, we did associate every now and then in class. I had a crush on Loco back then and we even talked for a hot lil second till Asha started showing interest in him. Sad thing is as much as I talked about Loco to her she never once said she liked him; it was always he looks ok he ain't all that.

Funny how as soon as I get the courage to talk to him this hoe wants him. So yea, I'm in my feelings and I went after her man because technically he was mines from the get-go and the bitch took him from me; that's how I feel. She living the life I should have had and have the nerves to flaunt it in my face and act like she ain't did shit wrong. I have been planning this revenge since she stabbed me in the back and snatched him away from me. SHE TOOK MY HAPPILY EVER AFTER!!!

As the time went on I paid attention to their every move. See Gary, IN is so small everyone knows everyone so it was easy to keep tabs on them. I knew every hang out Loco hung at, where he did his dirt, and every trap house he had. I even knew when they were on bad terms which usually led to Loco cheating on her or when he was drunk and put his hands on her. As you can see, I did my homework, so I knew it was just a matter of time when she will piss him off so bad it will be hard for him to just forgive her. That was when I will make my move which just so happens to be when she burnt up his precious car. BINGO right on target, so I knew I had to stake my claim and he will be down to get someone's pussy, and it was going to be mines.

That night he came into the club was the night I got my revenge on Asha. It was a long time coming but the wait was well worth it. They say good things comes to those who wait. And I waited long enough. Now I'm having his baby and it's going to be a life or death situation before I let her have him and before I let him walk away from me or our lil family. And since she put her hands on me and could have made me lose my baby, putting sugar in her gas tank is just not enough for me. This bitch just messed my face up and I'm a fine ass bitch. Hell, I need my face and body to make my paper and she made me lose two weeks of pay by putting her hands on me. It was only right that I returned the favor and made her lose her paper as well by not having a vehicle to get to work in. Now all I need to do is catch this hoe slipping and slice and dice her pretty little face up; we'll see if Loco wants her ass then.

Yes, I can admit Loco has told me he will never leave Asha and he loves her. So after that night went down he cut off all communication with me and he stopped fucking me. The last time I saw him was when I was getting into the ambulance that night it all went down. So when the doctor came in and told me I was expecting I couldn't help but smile and think to myself that this was the best revenge ever. He was most definitely going to be a part of my life forever and I wasn't ever going anywhere. I called Loco for almost a month straight and even text him and no response. I really didn't want to let him know I was pregnant over a text but needless to say he left me with no choice.

I text Loco and just plain out said I found out I was 14 weeks pregnant the night your bitch jumped on me. At that point, he responded immediately and said, "Are you serious?" Instead of me replying to him, I sent a picture of the hospital paperwork.

He responded saying, "Damn so what are you going to do?"

"Now I'm currently 19 weeks pregnant and there is no way in hell I will get an abortion so you need to talk to me because your about to be a dad."

"I will be right over." And just like that it was the first communication we had since. Now he did keep his word and came right over for us to talk about our new bundle of joy.

"So Cinnamon what the hell you gone do because I can't have no baby by you. Hell Asha find this shit out she really ain't gone take me back. Besides I'm not ready or trying to be no daddy man. What the fuck."

"Well Loco first off I can care less about a damn Asha and her finding out. Second of all I'm having this baby and you are the father so get over it because whether you're ready or not, it's happening, and you should've thought about all that before you were knocking my back out without a condom."

"Bitch who the fuck you think you talking to like that first of all? Second of all, it's strange how your ass was so willing to fuck me without a condom the first night. Your hoe ass probably set me up and that probably ain't even my baby." All I can think about was him saying I set him up. Well he was right about the setup part but I didn't try to get pregnant on purpose.

"Oh really nigga? It ain't your baby and now I'm hoe? Yea ok. I wasn't a hoe when you were all up inside me nutting so freely or sneaking around with me behind Asha's back. Nor was I a hoe when you were with me damn near every night your bitch ass couldn't stay out this pussy or leave me alone so who seems to be the hoe?"

Loco looked at me like he wanted to blow my brains out. I knew me mentioning Asha's name pushed one of his buttons and that was a line I crossed that would get me put six feet under. At this point in time I really didn't care. I was tired of this whole Asha situation and I was going to eliminate her out of the picture for good. Hell I'm the one carrying his damn child so I deserved to be in the picture once and for all.

"Cinnamon keep fucking playing with me I'mma fuck your lil ass up. You lucky you're pregnant."

"Boy please. Regardless if I was pregnant or not, you ain't gone do shit. The only thing you will be fucking up over here is this pussy so miss me with that shit. Hell I ain't Asha."

Now me and Loco always argued but his bitch was never brought up and usually when we argued it led to some rough hot sex which was just what I needed at the time. Being pregnant heightened my hormones to the highest extent. Not to mention I was already a freak but now it seems as if I'm 10x's freakier than usual. Now as soon as I finished my sentencing Loco grabbed me by my neck and threw me on the bed trying to choke the shit out of.

I have no clue why this turned me on even more so I proceeded to massage his long big juicy dick and felt all of his manhood extend in my hand. From that point on, I knew it was on. H instantly released his grip from my neck and got to tonguing me down and massaging my clit. We instantly got to ripping one another's clothes off and I grabbed all 12" of him and took him into my mouth. I sucked and slobber all over his dick like it was my last meal, had his toes curled up and his eyes rolling in the back of his head. Once I took his long, black, juicy dick and his balls into my mouth, he let out a big ass moan and grabbed the back of my head to push me down further on his dick.

"Damn Cinnamon baby shit. Suck that shit girl!!!" With that being said, I picked up my pace and sucked harder and faster and stroked him with my hand all at the same time.

Once I did that Loco couldn't take it anymore. He flipped me over and began to flick his tongue over my clit, fucking me with his tongue. That shit felt so good I couldn't keep my composure. My pussy instantly started to throb and my clitoris started swelling. I was moaning so loud and gripping the sheets so tight all Loco can say was come on and come for daddy baby. And at his command, I came like he left the water on and the sink was overflowing. He smirked and said, "yea that's what I'm talking about and pushed his dick up inside me so fast and so hard I screamed and clawed at his back. This was my punishment for crossing the line; I know but I was loving every single thrust that man gave me.

He punished my pussy till I literally could not take it anymore. My shit was so sore and so dry it felt raw. Hell he even ripped me because it stings a lil when I use the bathroom. I have to say I have never been fucked like that in my life and I for damn sure never had a dick that big so I guess it's safe to say I was sprung on him and his dick.

As soon as I left the bathroom and came back into the room the first thing Loco said is, "I bet next time you will watch your mouth or else it will be worse than that and next time I won't show you mercy." Then he turned over and went to sleep on my ass.

I woke up to him cussing at the phone and I had no clue to what was going on so I asked him and surely wasn't expecting him to say, "Asha not answering the phone or responding to my text."

Seriously after the night we just had he is really still on this Asha shit. You have a whole baby on the way and she is still the only thing that is crossing this niggas mind. Yea, I have to do something about her and do something fast, because this shit is really pissing me off. And from that point on, I started to put my plan in place to get rid of my headache that jeopardized my family once and for all. Loco was going to lead me right to her and she would not even know what hit her.

For the remainder of the day, he continued to call her and text her and never got a response, so he grew more and more irritated. He even called her cousin Autumn which in turn made him get angrier since she hadn't heard from Asha either. I watched his every move because I knew in time he will leave and go to her house and at that time I will follow him to stake my target. Truth be told I didn't have to even touch her to get her to leave him alone. All I had to do was tell her I'm pregnant. but just as I thought, he tells me he's going to check on Asha and yes of course I got an attitude but I played it cool.

Loco jumped into his car and I followed him in mine. He never even knew I was behind him since I waited till he was at the stop sign before pulling off. Following him, I noticed we were headed towards *Dorie Miller,* and I thought he must not be going to Asha's house; she is the last person I thought will stay in the PJs. To my surprise, she really does stay out there because as soon as we pulled up, I see her walking out the house with the twins and her cousin Autumn. I turned to look in Loco's direction, because I knew that some shit was about to jump off and I didn't know whether to watch or run because all I seen was Loco pull out his 9 mm and both twins pulled out their 40cal, while everyone else got to screaming.

Chapter 6-When the Shit Hits the Fan

Asha

Now I can't believe this shit here!!! After I told his dumb stupid ass I'm done he has the nerve to steady keep showing up at my house unexpected like he owns something over here. Mind you we live in the fucking PJs and this can cause us to get kicked the hell out. Everybody running, ducking, and screaming all over the fact they seen some damn guns and not one bullet has been let out. Maybe because I stood in the middle of them along with Autumn; there was no way in hell we were about to let this shit go down.

"Loco what the fuck are you doing here? "

"Oh so that's all you can say? Explain to me what the fuck this bitch ass nigga doing here and why you ain't been answering the damn phone?"

It dawned on me that I still hadn't returned anyone's calls or texts, and my phone was still on do not disturb mode all this time.

"Okay for one, all y'all need to lower your guns. People are about to call the police and Loco you know damn well you're not even supposed to be out here so you will go straight to jail."

"I'm not lowering shit till this nigga take that gun off my brother." Well, I can understand where Dru was coming from, so I couldn't be mad at him for that, but damn, these niggas supposed to be cool and they upping strap on one another like they ain't never kicked it in broad daylight.

"Okay Loco put down your gun. There is nothing going on between me and Dre."

Loco just looked at me like I was crazy then Dre said, "Yea dude, listen to your girl cuz ain't shit happen."

Right then and there something must have clicked in his stupid ass brain cuz he lowered his gun. I can tell Dre really wanted to beat his ass right then and there and was mad as hell. Autumn was so shocked and scared she just started crying right where she stood and Dru had to carry her back in the house along with escorting Dre in the house as well.

"Asha I'm sorry; I didn't mean to cause all this drama. It's just I got worried when you didn't answer the phone and I was coming to check on you then to see y'all together I snapped. I was wrong my bad."

"Now see I don't know what part of I don't want nothing else to do with you that you don't understand, so my well-being and who I'm fucking is none of your concern Loco. We're through, done, over with."

"Asha you know damn well we will never be through and as far as who your fucking it will always be my concern cause if you ain't fucking me you ain't fucking no damn body. A nigga will have to kill me before I let that shit happen because I'm most definitely going to kill his ass."

Right then and there I knew I needed to move again and this time no one was going to know where I lived. This shit had seriously hit the fan and I saw that murderous look in his eyes so I knew he was serious. The only way he was going to leave me along completely is if one of us was dead and I be damn if that's me. I stood there for a while and just looked at him with complete disgust, shook my head, and walked away.

"I'm not playing with your ass Asha. That's my pussy and you know it, so play with it if you want to. Both y'all will be fucked up!!!"

Yea I see this nigga done lost his marbles real talk. I ignored him and got in my car and pulled off on his ass. I was furious; so furious all I seen was red and really wanted to blow his head back. As of right now the way my blood was boiling, if death do us part is what he wanted then death do us part is what he will get. As I'm in deep thought, my phone rang and the caller ID displayed Moe's name. Can this day get any weirder?

Without meaning to, I answered the phone with a complete attitude, "What!!"

"Well hello Miss Lady. Did I catch you at a bad time? Is everything okay with you?"

"I'm sorry; I didn't mean that. I just went through some bullshit not too long ago but I'm cool what's up?"

"You sure cuz you been M.I.A for about two days now."

"Yes Moe. I'm good. Just needed some time to myself and ain't want to be bothered that's all. And I haven't had the chance to return everyone's calls or text yet that's all."

"Okay well that's understandable. You said you just went through something a few minutes ago so I take it you need to clear your head. How about you meet me at *Miller Beach* so we can talk and you can just clear your brain."

"Sounds cool; I need to get myself together anyway before work so I guess I will see you in like fifteen minutes."

After ending the call, I headed towards the beach and got there way before him because I was already close by, which was good because it gave me ample time to check all my messages and return calls that needed to be returned. I finished all my calls and texts just in time because Moe had just pulled up. Now he is the last person I really needed to be around at a time like this but I really needed to clear my head. He was just the right distraction for me to do that. Now don't get me wrong, I'm not down for fucking him even though I wanted to but I'm a lady first and foremost. Admiring his sexiness will make any bitch forget about what happened thirty minutes ago. Hell, he will make you forget the last three minutes if you ask me.

I never expected for him to go all out and have a whole picnic scene going on; I only expected us to talk. This nigga came with blankets, food, wine, and roses. I have to say I was really impressed… so impressed I had to play it off and ask him what was this supposed to be because I didn't agree on a date. He couldn't do nothing but laugh and responded by saying, "Shorty, I don't know about you but a nigga gotta eat and that's one way for me to clear my head." Now I have to admit he do have a point so picnic it is.

Me and Moe sat and talked for hours about any and everything that I lost track of time. I really have to say I enjoyed myself and he took my mind away from any and all negativity that had occurred. It's crazy that we have so much in common and enjoy doing a lot of the same things. He was nothing, but a true gentleman and I hated ending the evening with him but of course a Sista got to make her paper. I couldn't help but think about Moe the rest of the night while I was at work. He is really starting to rub off on me since I'm noticing that there is more to him than just what meets the eye. Like they say you should never judge a book by its cover. His personality is way sweeter, than his street, dope boy ways.

After that night, me and Moe began to get real close and started spending more and more time together. Now I have to admit, I wasn't ready to be in a relationship and I still have my guard up. My trust level for any nigga is slim to none but I loved his company, and as of now, he was the only thing keeping me sane and keeping a smile on my face. I had moved out of me and Autumn's house in *Dorie Miller* and left the house to Autumn and Dru since he moved in. I was now living in Valparaiso, IN which is like thirty-five minutes away from Gary.

I tried my best to stay away from Gary after all that mess that happened with Loco and the twins. The only time I was in sight was school and work. Of course Autumn wasn't too happy I moved but she clearly understood why. She hated the fact I moved way in Valpo cause no one from the hood goes there yet that was my main reason for heading in that direction. Last place anyone would look for me at especially Loco. I had a three story house with four bedrooms, two full baths, a half bathroom in the basement, and a three car garage.

Me and Autumn haven't been kicking it as much as we did since I moved and I haven't been around the rest of the ladies that much either. Seems like all I do now is go to school, eat, sleep, work. Hell, come to think of it, I barely talked on the phone and went out. I guess this is why the girls made this weekend a sleepover at my new place so we can all catch-up. They realized the change and the distance in me before I did so they wanted to make sure everything with me is okay. I have to say the past two months have been a little lonely without them and I'm missing my girls so I can't wait for this weekend.

Autumn had the whole housewarming/sleepover theme put together and she organized the whole thing. I been a homeowner for two months now and the only people who has been to my home is my dad and Autumn when I first moved in. I hired movers to move me in because of the distance and I didn't want to take the chance of Loco finding anything out. So yes it was well past time to bring the girls over and have a ladies' night. As I was getting up to prepare for the ladies' arrival the phone rang and to my surprise it was Netta.

"Hey girl how is you, long time no hear from?"

"Hey Netta how did you get this number?"

"Don't be mad Asha, but I went and visited your dad and he gave it to me on the promise my brother wouldn't get a hold of it and trust me he won't be able to contact you but I really needed to talk to you."

"Okay now Netta you said that the last time when I moved you wouldn't give him my info and you did which resulted in him coming there causing chaos and pulling a gun out on the twins. Now I just got my number changed; I really don't want to change it again so please don't give it to him."

"Girl trust me; I won't. He will never even know I contacted you especially after what I just found out and the reason why I called you."

After hanging up the phone with Netta and learning that Loco got Cinnamon pregnant I felt like the whole world just came crashing down on me all over again. Everyone has tried their hardest to keep any and all news about Loco away from me. The last time I seen him was when he pulled a gun out on the twins and he came to my school a few days after that but was immediately escorted off the premises before he could even approach me. I was moved out of the house already the last time Autumn told me he popped up over there and he stormed off when he was told I no longer lived there. She closed the door in his face before he could question her any further. Now here it is his sister done resurfaced him back into my mind when I haven't thought about him in all this time and I was finally getting over everything.

I continued to just lay there with all this going on in my head. I knew Netta didn't mean any harm with letting me know; she actually thanked me for getting myself out of the situation before things got bad cause knowing me, if we were still messing around, I would be in jail finding this out. Especially since Netta said Cinnamon is like 28 weeks along. I got even more mad and was even more heartbroken knowing he got her pregnant during the time we were still together and living together, which in turns mean he probably got her pregnant in our house and bed. Thinking about that alone made me break down in tears. Hell I was so hurt; this whole time we were together we never thought about having kids till we were married yet he gets this thot pregnant.

I ended up crying myself to sleep when in actuality, I was supposed to be getting prepared for ladies' night. But now all I wanted to do was curl up in a ball, cry, and be left alone. Even though I felt that way, I couldn't let his actions take me back to that place. Besides the ladies were already ringing the doorbell.

The first thing that came out of Coco's mouth when she seen me was, "Damn bitch, you sleep? All you do is sleep. Is your ass pregnant or something?" Everyone got quiet and looked at me waiting for an answer wondering if it's a possibility. Hell to tell you the truth I needed to know myself because come to think of it, I haven't had a period in two months. Of course, I told them I wasn't and informed them what had occurred. I didn't get a chance to cook and get the liquor so we ordered pizza and Meka went to get drinks; the girls made sure to keep my mind away from Loco yet I couldn't help but wonder if I was pregnant or not.

Chapter 7- Acceptance

Loco

So, it's been two months since I saw or talked to Asha. I finally came to the realization that we were done for good this time. Even tough that was the last thing I wanted, I knew it was over. Hell, she done sat here and uprooted her whole life to Lord knows where to get away from me and changed her number. Plus, I had to accept the fact that Cinnamon was seven months pregnant with my twins and there was no denying that.

Don't get me wrong, I still was in love with Asha and really wanted to be with her but at the same time I had to realize that maybe after all we been through I'm not what's best for her. Since I couldn't be with her, I will always be there for her and didn't want to lose our friendship. I have been trying to contact her just to let her know that I was sorry and to inform her about Cinnamon being pregnant, yet when I tried to do that, I was escorted off the premises at her school so I decided to leave well enough along. I guess when the time is right we will meet up. Till then, I have to focus on being a dad.

Me and Cinnamon decided on moving in together since I gave up the house me and Asha had together. Things didn't seem right being or living there without her. Too many memories; plus, Cinnamon didn't want to ever go back to that house after Asha put them hands on her. Now don't think just because I live with this bitch and she carrying my seed we about to get married and shit. Naw that shit ain't about to shake. I still did my thang and was still, as she will say, "a hoe" in her terms. And in my mind the only female that was worthy enough to wear my last name was Asha.

Of course, Cinnamon thought she had me to that point. I figured out, that all this shit was a setup from the start. Of course, she wasn't aware that I had found that information out from her journals she kept over the years. So I knew she wasn't done trying to get Asha out of my life for good. We all know that will never happen and if it came down to it, baby momma or not, I will kill her ass if she ever put Asha in harm's way.

Cinnamon was cool though and she was a down ass chick willing to do whatever whenever for her man. Yea, I cared for her in a sense of her being my kids' mother so I was there to work things out with her to raise our kids together. The only thing was that my heart was not with her and that's what she wanted. She been at me since middle school even when I was with Asha. That's why in her mind Asha took me from her but that was never the case.

I always had a crush on Asha, but back then, I was scared to say something, so I had my sister hook us up since they were cool. It just so happens my sister did it at the time Cinnamon told me how she felt about me and we talked on the phone a few times. It was nothing like what she thought and we were never a couple, but I guess in her mind, phone conversations make you a couple. Now because of this, I'm trapped dealing with this for the rest of my life all over a middle school crush. I sit back every day wondering and asking myself how I got myself into this shit. Why the fuck did I let my dick think for me and not my heart and head?

Well fuck it; it is what it is, and hell, Cinnamon's pussy was one of her best qualities anyway. Shorty knew how to work that shit, and it got even better with her being pregnant. Don't get me wrong, my baby momma not ugly, but hell besides pussy, and her okay looks, she doesn't have an education or shit going for herself. Hell, she stripped for a living which was one thing we fought about all the time. She hated when I would tell her that if she wants to take Asha's place, then she needs to be like her and do something for herself. She can't swing around a pole pregnant

. The first time I said that she threw a glass ashtray at my head and missed so I laughed at her stupid ass which pissed her off even more.

As you can see, I love pissing her the fuck off because every time we argued or fight we have that good ass makeup sex. Sometimes I think she do shit on purpose to get a reaction out of me to make me say some slick shit to her to start a fight. She liked that rough sex shit and never let me take my time with her which is what

I wanted to do considering she bout to pop, but somehow shit always ended up as me pounding her shit like it was no tomorrow.

"Hey Asha, I mean, my bad, Cinnamon get your ass up and cook something. Shit, a nigga hungry as hell. All you do is sit your lazy ass down around here and don't do shit!!!"

"Hold up, Bitch! Did you just call me Asha? Do I look like a fucking Asha to you hoe!!!"

"Bitch, who the fuck you calling a bitch? Bitch!! And you the hoe, you came onto me, remember, while I was in a relationship, which screams THOT all day!!"

"Well then, since I'm a thot then this thot doesn't need to cook your damn food so how bout you make the shit yourself or be hungry for all I give a fuck! How about that?"

Once she said that I knew exactly how to handle her. So I walked to the kitchen where she was and she had her back turned to me. I walked over to her and instantly bent her over the countertop.

See I had easy access to the pussy because she has a tendency to not wear undies and all she had on was a T-shirt. While I'm bending her over, I got one hand on her neck and the other hand I used to massage her clit. Her juices instantly ran down my hand with one single touch. Shorty was ready for her daddy to enter her paradise.

I slowly took the tip of my dick and rubbed it up and down her pussy. She instantly let out a moan which only turned me on even more. I gently entered her and her pussy started to convulse around my dick like it was trying to suck me all the way in.

"Ooooh Daddy give it to me right there!!"

"Um yea, you like that huh? You like daddy's dick?"

"Yes Daddy. I love that dick."

"So your ass gone cook?"

"Yes papi."

"You gone clean?"

"Ummm, baby yes, yes, yes."

And just like that, she came all over my dick and made a big ass puddle on the kitchen floor too, so I smacked her on her ass and told her to clean that shit up and have my food done by the time I got out the shower. She nodded her head in agreeance and I went on to jump in the shower. See I had to get ready and meet my fellows to pick up our work that night. We had a few trap houses that needed a couple of kilos, and we also needed to collect on them as well. Business was a little slow nowadays, since that nigga Moe was trying to take over, of course.

That reminded me, why in the fuck was this hoe ass nigga over Asha crib? Was he trying to get to her to get to me? This nigga been trying to take over my little territory for the longest. See my section of Gary was the only section this nigga ain't have and he wanted it bad. So the blood between us was toxic as hell. He done even went as far as having us set up and robbed a few times thinking that was gone scare us off. Naw, that shit ain't work. Ain't no hoes over this way. We been on this block for far too long to let this nigga from the Chi come in and do a takeover. This my city… my hood, and we gone ride or die for our set.

When I thought about it, I realized this nigga will do anything to get at me to try and take over my set, and everybody in these parks know about me and Asha, so I'm sure it done got back to him that Asha was my girl. Question is will he try and put Asha in harm's way just to get at me and try to prove a point? See now this shit got me bugging, and by any means necessary, I have to protect Asha. But how the fuck can I do that when I don't even know where the fuck she lives?

Shit, I instantly grabbed my shit, called my nigga Tone up and told him to meet me at the spot. We had some shit to handle. Headed out the crib, Cinnamon asked did I want my plate. She ended up making tacos so I took it with me. I arrived at the spot at the same time Tone did. I told him what was going on with this nigga Moe and informed him about the possibility that Asha might be in danger.

Once Tone was informed, he rounded up all the fellas to be on the lookout for Moe to protect Asha.

The one person I knew that can get a hold of Asha better than I can at this point was my sister Netta, so I called her to inform her of the issue. I didn't want Asha to be scared but I did want her to know that it was a possibility. I knew Asha knew how to handle her own and she was capable of blowing any nigga rocks back if it came down to it, yet I didn't want her to be in this predicament over me so the best thing for me to do was knock this nigga off before he gets me or the love of my life.

Chapter 8- The Arrival

Cinnamon

So lately me and Loco been bumping heads a lot and he always trying to throw this Asha bitch in my face. Frankly, it was getting on my nerves. If I wasn't eight months pregnant, I would have to go in his mouth. It's been plenty of times this nigga had the nerve to even call me Asha. Yea, that's right, he called me Asha, and I bet the first thing you're thinking is how am I still fucking with him right? Well, for the most part, I didn't go through all this trouble just to walk away, and on top of that, I am having two kids by him at one time.

Besides, the way I see it, I still won. I guess your wonder how I figure that, because he still loves Asha right? Let's see, I'm the one he is with, he lives with, and of course, I have his first kids. Plus, I get that dick on a regular. This nigga ain't going nowhere. He can never leave this pussy along. Even if he did try, and I mean try to go back to Asha, I'm still in his life forever, and I wouldn't let this nigga leave that easily. Once I drop this load, he will be madly in love with me and his kids and that hoe will be a none factor.

Speaking of dropping the load, I have been contracting since eight o'clock this morning and Loco is nowhere to be found. It is now close to noon so I'm left with calling his sister Netta, which I hate, because me and this bitch do not get along. Mind you, she is cool with Asha and she even had the nerve to ask me for a DNA test when she found out I was pregnant to make sure it's her brother's baby. The nerve of her, right? Did she actually think I would plot all these years to make him mines just to turn around and get knocked up by some other random dick. Yea the fuck right. I don't have shit to hide so I agreed to a blood test to satisfy everyone. Plus, it's proof to rub in Asha's face.

Anyway, Loco's ass finally called and told me he would meet me at the hospital; he apologized for taking so long to get back to me. He said he had to handle something that is causing a threat to him. I had no clue what that was about and decided not to get into it because my contractions were coming stronger and stronger and kicking my ass. I arrived at the hospital by ambulance and went straight to Labor and Delivery. Loco came straight up and they started to get me prepped to have an emergency cesarean, because I was having two kids at one time and one of them was breeched.

I gave birth to a boy and a girl. My son weighed five pounds, one ounce, and my daughter weighed five pounds even. My son, Stef'Vaugh, was born first at 2:30 pm, and six minutes later, Serenity was here. Loco stood right by my side the whole time smiling and snapping pics. I was able to stay up during the procedure and it was a joy to hear my babies cry. For them to be born a month early, they were healthy as hell. The doctor didn't see a reason to keep them in the ICU or an incubator.

Right when I got to my room after the delivery, Loco waited long enough for the twins to get their body temperature right and be able to come into the room. Of course, he had to help me hold them due to my surgery, because I was very sore. Once I laid eyes on them and was able to nurse them with the help of the nurse, he said he would be back within another hour or two. He kissed the twins and walked away without giving me a kiss goodbye or anything. *Really though? I just had your kids and you walk out to run the street instead of bonding with your twins? Where the fuck do they do that at?*

Once I learned how to breastfeed the twins and got them situated, I had them to take them back to the nursery, so I could get some rest. I was in a lot of pain from my incision, and she had just given me pain medicine. I didn't want to take the chance of falling asleep with the twins being in the room and they start crying and I couldn't get to them. Besides Loco wasn't here to help me with them. An hour had already passed since Loco had been gone, so I text him to let him know I was taking a nap. I also asked him when he would be back to help me tend to the kids. I fell asleep before I could get an answer from him.

I ended up taking a two-hour nap and was awoken to the nurse bringing the twins in for a feeding. I looked at my phone and noticed I still did not have a text from Loco. While feeding the kids, I started flipping through the channels and came across the news with Loco's picture plastered all over the news.

"What the fuck? Ain't this about a bitch!!!" The nurse quickly came running back into my room at the sound of me yelling.

"Ma'am, is everything okay? Are you in any pain or anything?"

"No I'm not. My baby daddy is on the news. Can you please take the twins for me so I can see what's going on?"

"Yes, no problem. I will take them back to the nursery."

I instantly grabbed my phone once the nurse walked out with my kids. I called Netta to see what happened, and all she could tell me was she just found out herself while she was on her way to the hospital to see the kids so she made a detour to go to the police station.

All we know is that he was at one of his spots and it got raided. Out of all this time Loco done had these spots, they never been raided. Hell, you would've never known that they were spots. They were real low-key with their shit so we already knew it was some setup type of shit. Shit seemed real iffy right about now. Not to mention his spots had got robbed a few weeks ago and they took a loss but not a big loss, which is what the robbers wanted. Listening to the news seems like they raided every single one of his spots and all of his workers and his right-hand men are gone to jail.

While watching the news trying to get more information, my phone rings and scared the shit out of me.

"You have a collect call from 'Loco', an inmate at Lake County Correctional facility. To accept this call, press one." I pressed one before the operator was able to finish the rest of her sentence and was immediately connected to him.

"Hello, bae what the hell happened? You're all on the news and shit; all y'all."

"Man, that nigga Moe set us up. You know he want them spots. Plus, when they were bringing us out the crib, the nigga was standing across the street smiling and shit."

"Wow, so what are they saying? This some bullshit. We just had twins, and you only seen them for a few hours since they been in the world."

"Yea, Cinnamon damn! Don't you think I know that shit? Hell, I was on my way back to the damn hospital when the shit happened. I had bought baby clothes and all the shit is still in the car."

"So where is the car and your sister is at the jailhouse already."

"Yea I know; I just released my belongings to her, and the car is still parked across the street. Hell, I'm good. They don't have shit on me. There was nothing in the crib but a gun so I'm only gone be in here for the weekend since today is Friday. I will go in front of the judge Monday."

"Okay, well I'm supposed to get released from the hospital on Sunday, so I can make it to court and I got bail money if needed."

"Alight, my sister has instructions on what needs to be done, and she will be up there to bring the twins' things. She will be going to get the car. Kiss my kids for me."

With that being said, we ended the call and Netta was walking into the room with gifts. "Hey girl, where are my niece and nephew?"

"Hey, I sent them to the nursery when I seen the news. Let me call and have them bring them back down."

So I bet you wondering how did me and his sister get cool right? Well in actuality we're not cool, but we tolerate one another on the account I am her brother's baby momma and we are together.

Like I said from the start, I had nothing to hide. I did the DNA test while I was still pregnant before the twins got here and just like I thought, he was 99.99999999% the father. Once she seen that she couldn't do nothing but respect it and accept it. Hell their mother even came around and also offered to throw the baby shower for the twins once they got here. See all we knew was we were having twins. I didn't want to know the sex till they were here so the baby shower would of course be based upon their arrival. As the nurse was bringing the twins in, Loco and Netta's moms was coming in right behind her.

"Hello you guys. How are my grandbabies?"

"Hello. They're okay."

"And how are you Cinnamon considering the circumstances? Are you okay? Do you need help?"

"Well yes, because I still can't move around that good so I have to send the twins back and forth to the nursery. I just had them six hours ago and now this."

"Well, I can understand that. I guess me or Netta can take turns spending the night up here to help out. When do you get released?"

"Hopefully Sunday."

"Well mom, Loco's court date is Monday, so do you think you can keep the twins so me and Cinnamon can go to his court hearing?"

"Why of course Netta. I can finish getting things ready for the welcome home baby shower anyway."

"Okay, well I guess I will have the first night here at the hospital, and mom you take tomorrow."

With arrangements made so I can have help with the twins, I went to sleep since it wasn't time for their feedings and their granny and aunt had them. All this excitement in one day was too much for me to handle. I was mentally and physically drained. I was very grateful that his family stepped up to help even though we don't see eye to eye. They really don't care much for me. They let me know and showed me they will be there for my kids, and that was all I needed. I did not expect much from them because deep down I knew they were all for Asha and felt some type of way about me and how I ended up with Loco to begin with. In their eyes, I was a homewrecker, but oh well, I was in this for me.

It was Monday, a day that I wasn't truly not ready for. I didn't know what this judge was going to do and I was not prepared to take care of these twins without Loco. As of right now, I was all in my feelings while trying to pump my milk and get ready for court. Loco's mom was downstairs with the twins getting them dressed for the day. I managed to get four bottles of milk, two for each child right before Netta pulled up. Walking into that courtroom, I felt like the world was about to end seeing him in his orange jumpsuit. It really broke my heart listening to the judge give him a bond of twenty thousand dollars for one-gun charge. That just made me break down. Where was I going to get eighteen thousand dollars from? I expected it to be a simple bond if any bond, but ten percent of twenty thousand. It's only one person who can bond him out with that amount of money and that was Asha.

Chapter 9- Caught Up

Asha

Well after the ladies' night session I still didn't bother to find out if I was pregnant or not. I just went on about my business like the convo was never brought up. That was a month ago and now here I am at the clinic getting tested. I haven't had a period in three months and the last thing I wanted was to let me and Loco goodbye sex end up having me pregnant; that wasn't goodbye… that was hello new chapter. I don't know what I'm going to do if this test comes back positive. I don't believe in abortions; yet I don't want kids right now especially not with Loco. Hell he just had twins this past weekend. Plus, he is now in jail. I'm so lost and this is the first time I have been lost and undecided on what to do when it came down to my life.

"Miss James, the doctor will see you now." The nurse said breaking me up out of my trance while I was sitting in the waiting room. She escorted me to this small room right off the nurses' station and handed me a cup to pee in. I have so much going through my mind right now all I can do is cry and pray that this test isn't positive. After peeing in the cup and returning back to my room, the phone rings and it's Netta out of all people.

"Hello, Netta this a bad time right now. Can I call you back?"

"Hey Asha, I need a favor right fast. It will only take two seconds to ask."

"Okay, what is it?"

"Well I know you heard about Loco, and even though you're probably the last person to ask, we need your help to bond him out." As soon as she said that, the doctor walks in.

"I'll call you right back Netta." I ended the phone before she could respond.

"Hello Miss James. I'm doctor Yang, and I will like to say congratulations. You are expecting."

Right then and there it felt like I was having a nervous breakdown or something. All my breath in my body left. *How can I have a baby? I still have one semester left in nursing school and I want nothing to do with the father. How can this happen to me right when I walk away for good? Out of all these years I never been pregnant by Loco?* The doctor had me lay back while she performed an ultrasound. I was exactly fourteen-and-a-half weeks along. I listened to my baby's heartbeat and all, and she printed out a pictures of the baby.

Leaving the doctor's office, I texted Netta to let her know I will help. As of now, I had no choice because I needed to let Loco know I was carrying his child right after he just had twins by the bitch he cheated with. Netta text me back and thanked me. She asked when did I want to meet up, and I told her she had to give me a minute. I would call her when I was ready. I was in need of some serious me time to collect my thoughts and cry and scream as much as needed.

Arriving home, all I could do was curl up in my bed and cry. I kept staring at the picture of my baby not wanting to believe this was my baby. I wasn't willing or ready to tell anyone just yet. I was still debating if I was going to tell Loco or if I was just going to hide it and keep it a secret. I also thought about taking my chances on going to Chicago to get an abortion. Who am I kidding? An abortion was out of the question. I don't even know why I thought about it from the start.

Don't get me wrong, I was capable of taking care of my child, but the thing was that I wasn't near bout ready for a baby. I have plans. I at least wanted to finish school and be established as a nurse for at least a year or two before I have anybody's baby. I also preferred to be married when I had kids. Yea, of course, I thought I was marrying Loco but that went out the window. Now everything is all messed up and screwed up. I also didn't plan on raising a child in Indiana either.

Thinking about my next move and how to handle my situation, I got a call from Moe. Now I haven't talked to him in a few weeks, especially after the information Netta told me about, which in turn, made me wonder about the situation Loco was now in. Then, out the blue, this nigga calls as soon as Loco gets locked up, and I find out I'm pregnant.

"What a motherfucking coincidence? You're calling me at a time like this."

"Well excuse me, Miss Lady. I was just calling to check on you since I haven't heard from you in a while and I wanted to make sure you were good?"

"Or are you calling to see what I know about Loco?" He instantly paused and took a deep breath. "Yea see, I know that the only reason why you're so interested in me is to get close to him. You want to use me to take him down or kill me to hurt him because you knew that was my nigga!!" He still hadn't responded which pissed me off even more. He basically just sat on the phone like he was puzzled or some shit. "Wow, ok. No response. So Moe, I'm going to put it to you like this. I'm not the one to be dealing with you and another nigga bullshit that I don't even fuck with anymore, so if you come for me be ready to put up one hellified fight."

With that being said, I ended the call and proceeded to text Netta to ask her about Loco's bond and inform her what just had happened with Moe. She informed me that they only wanted two thousand dollars which is ten percent of his actual bond, so they had enough to bond him out and thanked me for the willingness to help. She said that Cinnamon's dumb ass was going crazy thinking it would be a lot more and didn't understand how it actually worked. I let her know that I really needed to talk to her brother and to let him know it was important. She suggested I met them at the jail house since Cinnamon will stay at home with the twins, and she will be by herself.

I considered that will be the best option to talk to him without disclosing my phone number and where I lived. I told her to give me about an hour and I will text her when I'm headed to the jailhouse. After getting done texting Netta and making arrangements to meet, I still wasn't sure how I was going to tell Loco I was pregnant with his child. Hell, for that much, I wasn't even for sure if I was ready to tell him. I was still trying to tell myself for that matter. But at the end of the day, I knew it had to be done regardless so it was time for me to put on my big girl pants and face it head-on while I have the opportunity. I picked up the papers I got from the doctor stating I was pregnant and made a copy of it. I also grabbed one of my ultrasound pictures to give him the copy and the picture.

As soon as I was walking out the house, my phone rings. I looked down and it was Moe, now. After the conversation earlier, I have no clue what will make this man call me back so of course I ignored his call. I text Netta to let her know I was in route, and she responded that she was leaving out as well. I got to Lake County Jail House in thirty-five minutes, since I took the highway and Netta was already there bonding him out. I told her that I was not going to come in. I would wait in the car.

Netta came to the car saying it will be about an hour to an-hour-and-a-half for them to process him out so we can either leave and come back or wait here. I started to chicken out so I talked to Netta about the situation. Well actually I just showed her the paperwork and the ultrasound and told her to give it to him. I was going home.

"Hold up! Wait a minute, Bitch. How the fuck you just gone spring this up on me then try and walk away? Hell naw! We about to discuss this!!"

"Netta, I really don't want to talk. Hell I didn't even know how I was going to tell him. I'm still trying to process this."

"Wait Asha; when did you find out and how far along are you?"

"Well, I found out today, and I'm three months."

"Girl when did this happen? That night you broke it off completely huh?"

"Yes, the goodbye sex ended up being hello sex after all."

"Girl, I can't tell Loco this. It not for me to tell. You have to break that to him. It's not my place, but I'm happy as hell you about to have my niece or nephew."

"Don't you think I know this Netta? I know I have to tell him. I just don't know how and at least someone is happy and you do realize you have a niece and a nephew that was just born? That's another thing; he just had twins by a whole different female. How do I deal with being pregnant by him after all that?"

As soon as I said that, tears got to rolling out like a waterfall and I couldn't control myself.

"Awe Asha, I'm so sorry. Don't cry. Everything will be okay."

"How do you figure? this is not how this is supposed to be. I'm supposed to be his one and only; we were supposed to live happily ever after and get married. Not him get another bitch pregnant then knock me up on the side." As soon as I said that, we looked up to Loco walking up to us. I wiped my eyes and tried to contain myself.

"Hey y'all, what's going on? Is everything okay? Asha you good? Why are you crying?"

I handed Loco the papers without saying a word, jumped into the car, and pulled off before anyone of them could say something to me or try and stop me. I was crying so hard and had to pull over to get myself together. Plus, my tears clouded my vision. My phone was blowing up with calls and text messages from Netta, Loco, and Moe. Truthfully, Moe was blowing me up ever since I ignored his first call and now I have two more people added to the ignore section for the rest of the night. I admit I was upset that Netta would give Loco my number but considering the circumstances I knew it would be a matter of time for him to get the number anyway.

I decided to turn my phone off for the rest of the night but before I did that I read the last text that came through from Netta.

She said me and Loco really needed to talk and he was going crazy that I left like that. She also said she informed him about the Moe incident which made him wig out more. I text her back and said we would talk. I'm just not ready at this point. I thanked her and let her know I would talk tomorrow and that I was turning my phone off for the rest of the night.

From there, I turned my phone off and made my way home. As soon as I pulled onto my street, I noticed an unfamiliar car in front of my house. Mind you no one knows where I live, and this is not a car that I know so I stopped in the middle of the street contemplating on turning around or calling 911. As of now, all I could do was think about protecting my unborn child. I didn't know who this was, and if they caused a threat. I turned my phone back on and grabbed my 9 mm, making sure I had a bullet in the chamber. I proceeded to pull into my driveway and saw a figure sitting on my porch. I got out with my gun drawn and was greeted with a familiar voice that said, "Well hello, Miss Lady."

Chapter 10- The Truth

Loco

So, it seems this nigga Moe was at my head more than ever. I guess since he can't get Asha, he wants to try and set me up to go down in the pen, but lil did this clown ass nigga know that I'm twenty steps ahead of him. I will never be that stupid to leave my work in the crib after he done already had us robbed. I knew the next step was to try and knock me off or get me hemmed up, and that's exactly what he did, only for a petty ass gun charge though. I ain't sweating it, though. I got the best lawyer in the city, and I'm sure to get off this charge.

Now what I wasn't expecting was for Asha to be present when I walked out those doors and was released from jail. I damn sure wasn't expecting her to hit me with papers stating that she was pregnant. On top of that, she just threw them in my face and scurried off like a bat out of hell. Then she won't answer the damn phone. How the fuck you hit a nigga off with some shit like that and won't even talk to them. Now what the fuck am I supposed to do? A nigga just had twins by a bitch who I don't want, and now the woman who has my whole heart and soul is also expecting. Damn man, shit just got real, for real though.

Now here it is, I get to go home and deal with this ignorant ass bitch and can't even fuck while I'm dealing with her whining ass, because this bitch just dropped twins by C-section and shit. Can this shit get any worse? DAMN!!!

"So Loco, how you feeling about Asha being pregnant, and what are you going to do?"

"Man, Netta for real though, I don't even know. This shit is so unexpected and at the wrong damn time, but truth be told, I would've preferred to have a baby by Asha any day than by Cinnamon ass."

"Oh shit nigga! What the fuck you gone do about Cinnamon? Are you gone tell her?"

"FUCK that bitch real talk. I can care fucking less about her ass. The only reason I'm dealing with her is for the sake of my kids. My heart is and will forever be with Asha."

"Yea, that may be true, but you have to have some kind of feelings for her. You got kids with her and she is your girl. Hell, you were bold enough to fuck up your relationship with Asha because of her."

"I care on account that that's my kids mother, but I'm not in love with her. Besides Netta, I can't think about this right now. I have to handle this nigga Moe so I can be around for my kids especially since this nigga on Asha ass now and she pregnant I ain't going, let me make these phone calls so I can handle this."

I called my nigga Tone up and let him know we need to roll up on one, our code for drive-by. Now that Asha was at risk. He agreed. Plus, due to the little setup movement he pulled, he was already hot. I told him I would meet him at Nate's crib once I showered and got this jailhouse stench off me. Nate's crib is where we keep all our heat at and suit up for war, and war is what this hoe ass nigga was gone get.

My sister dropped me off at the crib and of course soon as I walked in, Cinnamon greets me at the door nagging and asking me why I didn't call her when I got out.

"Like, damn bitch, why the fuck does it matter when I'm coming straight here any damn way?"

"Well, I mean I did just have your kids forty-eight hours ago and your little hoe was present. How I know you didn't try and sneak off with her?" I couldn't do nothing but shake my damn head at this silly ass little girl. I went to see and kiss my babies and take a shower. I laid Asha's pregnancy papers in the room on the dresser, and I was sure Cinnamon's nosey ass was going to go through my shit because it was up under my release paperwork. As soon as I was about to exit out the bathroom, here this bitch come busting through the door.

"What the fuck is this shit Loco?" she said waving the pregnancy papers in my face.

"What the fuck it looks like? I'm sure you know. Didn't you get the same damn papers?" I said with irritation.

"So why the fuck you got Asha's pregnancy papers for and you claim she won't even fuck with you like that?"

"Look girl, get the hell out my face with that nonsense. You know what it is. You knew what is was when you threw yourself at me so stop acting dumb hell. Why else do you think I got the damn papers? The same mother fucking reason I had your damn papers, and if you look at the due date, she damn near four months pregnant, so evidentially, that means I ain't had sex with her in that long." As soon as I said that, I walked passed this little hoe and she out of nowhere punch me in my damn mouth.

Now why the fuck she went and did that, I have no clue, because a nigga's reflexes was a motherfucker. Before I knew it, I had the little bitch by the neck and pinned up against the wall damn near ready to snap her neck till one of the twins woke up.

"Bitch, don't you ever in your life pull that shit again. I will beat your hoe ass and won't think twice about it. Now go see what the fuck is wrong with my shorty, and I will be back. I got business to handle."

And just like that, I left. I admit I did feel bad about putting my hands on shorty. Hell, she did just have surgery, and I hope I didn't bust none of her stitches and shit, but hell, the bitch had it coming by putting her hands on me first. She knew damn well we weren't even together like that for her to be tripping anyway.

On my way to Nate's crib, I tried to call Asha one more time and of course she still wasn't answering so I left her a text.

Me: **Hey Asha. I know you're mad at me for all I done, and I'm very sorry. I never meant to hurt you, but we really need to talk as adults about you being pregnant. Please contact me.**

After I sent the text, I called up my sister Netta and told her to try and get a hold of Asha for me. I needed to let her know that I am here for her and I wanted to do right for her and the baby. I am really trying to take responsibility and we need to talk. But of course she not answering the phone for my sister as well. Sad part is neither one of us knew where she lived so the best thing for me to do is head over to her cousin Autumn's crib once I got done handling this business.

I pulled up in front of Nate's crib, and as usual, Tone was already there with the rest of the crew down for whatever. See, this is why they were my day one niggas. I never had to question their loyalty, and when in need, they right there. So me, Tone, Nate, Breezy, J-Roc, Tre, and Snoop headed to the garage to put our game plan together to put this nigga Moe in the dirt. We knew all of the businesses he owned and decided to send the little nigga a warning first. Since it was a weekday, we knew the clubs weren't jumping and would be closed unless they were in there handling some business so we decided to torch *The Link Bar*.

Even though this is the club my sister and Asha and them go to on a regular, it was also one of Moe's big money spots, so we had to hit him where it hurts the most. Our next stop will be his strip joint called *Scores Indiana* right off of Melton Rd. This was the tricky part, because it's a strip club meaning they were open seven days a week and didn't close till three in the morning. Lucky for us, it was a little after 2 am and we all had on all black. Even our ride was black on black so it would be hard to be seen and get noticed. We sat across the street waiting on the parking lot to clear so we can make our move.

It was now 3:30 am and the coast was clear; we each had a can of gasoline to surround the whole entire building. There will be no way in and no way out so if someone was left up in that motherfucker they were good as gone. Within five minutes, the building was up in flames and we were back on the highway. While in route back to the spot, I was able to power back on my cell phone once we were clear of the crime scene. Come on now. You didn't think I will be that dumb and stupid to sit here and leave a trace of evidence that can put me at the scene of crime, now did you? And I bet you're saying I just made this nigga rich because he gets insurance money, huh. Well, considering this is arson, he won't get shit from the insurance company either, so he has no more legal income which means he is the next target for the FEDs.

Now, I got a call from my sister asking about the club being burnt down. Even though she knew it was us, I would never admit to it. She informed me that Asha finally text her and told her when she got home Moe was at her door and she didn't know how he got her address. She said that so far everything was cool. They were outside talking till he got the phone call about the club so they both were on their way there. I told her cool so are we then. I need to get Asha away from this nigga one way or another.

We pull up to Nate's crib to change clothes and cars and headed on over to *The Link Bar*. Me and my sister pulled up at the same time, and the crowd had already formed. Funny thing is, as soon as I get out the car and walk over to my sister, me and this nigga

Moe locks eyes and this nigga's phone rings. Asha spots us and nodded her head so my sister went over to talk to her. I guess this nigga got the call that his other club was burnt to the ground as well because the nigga got off the phone in rage and of course all hell breaks loose within a blink of an eye.

Chapter 11- Savage

Cinnamon

So, this nigga must have forgot who the hell he is fucking with for real. He really just sat here and put his hands on me and I just had his kids. And he thinks this shit cute and funny that this hoe is pregnant. Yea okay. They both got another thang coming because I be damned if this bitch has a damn baby. She still trying to stand in my way and get her some shine, but not this time hoe.

I'm the one and only baby momma this nigga gone have for the rest of his life. Call me crazy, psycho, whatever. I don't give a fuck. I'm tired of having to step aside for this punk ass bitch. The only way this baby will see the light of day is if I'm dead and gone. I refuse to let my kids share their dad, and he also not about to treat my kids different just because it's a baby by her.

Fuck this, I'm tired of getting my heart broken and going back and forth with this whole love triangle. I just need to call in a favor and finally have this bitch popped off. Then, Loco will have no choice but to love me and only me. Just as I was about to make my call, the news caught my attention. It flashed on the screen that two Gary, IN clubs had burned down and they believe that the incidents were connected

This has Loco written all over it, because both clubs belong to that dude Moe. Which made me wonder where the hell Loco was this time of night. It was four am and he was not home. To think about it, this nigga only seen his kids twice, when they were born, and when he walked in this house after getting released from jail. I immediately called him and all I got was his voicemail. *Okay so phone going straight to voicemail without ringing. Plus, it's taking him too long to respond to my text.*

Now this can only mean one thing because, at 4 o'clock in the damn morning, ain't shit open but legs and liquor stores, so I see I'm going to have to serve this nigga just like I'm going to have to serve his bitch he so heads over heels for. I don't understand why this man can't see he has a damn good woman right here in front of him that love him unconditionally and will do any and everything possible for him and to be with him. That's okay; he gone learn one way or another. I'm destined to get my happily ever after by any means necessary.

I guess the twins must have read my mind because they both instantly started to cry at the same time. As I'm in there changing one of their diapers, up pops the devil and walk in to feed the other twin, so I said to him with an attitude, of course, "Glad to see you finally have time to help me with them."

Of course he didn't respond; he just started to talk and play with Serenity while feeding her. After I changed Stef'Vaughn, I sat down next to Loco to feed him and we remained silent. It was like neither one of us existed to the other one, which became awkward.

After a while, I finally broke the silence and asked him what the deal was, and if he was just going to sit there like nothing ever happened.

"Damn Cinnamon, can a nigga spend some time with the twins without you nagging a nigga and shit? Hell, I only seen them twice. We can talk about that without being in the room with them."

Of course you know that pissed me off and I had a major attitude so I laid the baby down and stormed out the room. I have to say being angry makes you forget about being in pain because I haven't taken one pain pill the whole day and was up and about like I didn't even have a C-section. I know one thing. As soon as my body calmed down, those pains hit me like a fucking race horse and before I knew it I was knocked out.

I woke up to Loco giving me breakfast in bed which I thought was so sweet. He had already fed, changed, and clothed the twins and was getting the house together for a welcome home get together for our babies. In all actuality, I wasn't in the mood to be bothered with no one but it is what it is. I took another pain pill and started to help him with the preparations. He told me that he knew we needed to talk but asked if we can just get through the day without any confusions. I agreed because today was for the twins and not about us.

By the time I got out of the shower, all I heard in the background was Rhianna's song "Work":

Work, work, work, work, work, work

He said me haffi

Work, work, work, work, work, work!

He see me do me

That was my key that Netta and his mom had arrived and started cooking. I proceeded to get dress in my Ed Hardy summer dress. Since I still wasn't able to wear all my clothes, this was easy to put on and comfortable. Even though I was still swollen a little, I still looked good and still had a nice figure. I weighed 120 pounds, with a caramel complexion, hazel brown eyes, and I kept my hair in a short bob. Mind you, I am a stripper, so my body was right in all the right places, and I was built to the tee. Well, you had to be to handle the pole so this dress match all my curves in the right places. It also made my perky C-sized tits sit straight up at attention.

Man, I tell you I couldn't wait till my six weeks was up because looking at how fine I was in the mirror I made my own pussy wet so I was horny than a motherfucker. I turned around and noticed Loco standing in the doorway checking me out. He had a slight grin on his face and he said, "You look nice to just be dropping two kids at once." I couldn't help but blush and tell him thank you. I walked over to him to give him a kiss; I couldn't lie, he was fine as hell and with all this sexual tension I had built up, it made me feel like I was in heat so just a little kiss sent shocks to my little girl down there, and she was readier than a pot pie.

If I was in this much heat, I was sure he needed to release some tension as well, so with that being said, and being the good woman I am, I instantly went to work. Besides, I had a point to prove. I was on a mission to show him I was the one for him, and I needed to take his mind completely away from Asha. I grabbed his big masculine dick, pulled it out of his pants, and started massaging it. All he can say was, "Damn baby, stop starting shit. We have company and you just had surgery." And with that being said, I took all 12" in my mouth without hesitation.

"Oh shit! Damn Cinnamon. What the fuck? That shit feels so good." I had this nigga's eyes rolling in the back of his head and he was going crazy. Not to brag, but I must say my head game was on point. I was working the shit out his dick with my mouth while constantly massaging it with my hand as well. The faster I went, the louder the slurps got, and the tighter he gripped my head and pushed me down further.

"Awe shit! Awe shit, damn girl! I'm about to explode." And just like that, I sucked every single last drop out of him making sure not to miss a drop and swallowed it all like the champ I am.

He loved when I did that shit, and he knew he wasn't going to get that type of treatment anywhere else. We both fixed ourselves up to join the party since the guest were already starting to arrive.

Everyone was out back having them a good ole time; people was dancing, laughing, and of course, the food was smelling good with the grill still going. Me and him looked and smiled at each other like we were innocent, and I made note that the twins were in their car seats asleep by Netta. His mom threw on a throwback and grabbed her son to dance with him, and all you heard was Al Green's song "Love and Happiness":

Love and happiness

But wait a minute,

Something's going wrong

Someone's on the phone

This was Loco, and his mom's favorite song and they always danced together with this song. I remember watching Loco and his mom danced to this song when we were younger. I was amazed at all the family and friends we had over to welcome our new arrivals. We were all so happy and enjoying one another's company just like a family should. This was now my life and my happiness and nothing

or no one would come between it.

Chapter 12- Sweet Thang

Asha

Man, I swear I was about to let my whole 17 round clip off in his ass for sitting on my porch like that unannounced. He just didn't know what was coming to him, if I would have never recognized his voice by him saying Miss Lady. Of course he is the only one that calls me that but hell he was about to catch a hot one quick, fast, and in a hurry. I was always taught to shoot first ask questions later, and I stuck to that.

"Moe what the fuck are you doing here?" I said while still pointing the gun at his head.

"Well hello to you too. Can you lower the gun please? I'm not here to hurt you or cause you any harm. I'm here to talk to you. See, I will show you."

As he said that, he started to take off his shirt and turn around to let me see he wasn't strapped and he lifted up his pants legs too.

I was star struck just at the sight alone when he took off his shirt. Oh got damn, was all I can think about. Baby had one hellified body out this world and had all the cuts in all the right places. Shit, fuck a six-pack. This nigga had a twelve pack with a body like the model Chadoy Leon. This nigga looked just like his ass only with braids and even though this nigga could be shiesty as hell, I was sweet as shit on his ass and drooling like a dog. I had to clear my throat and lower my gun before this nigga noticed me noticing him. Mind you I had to keep it cute and simple like I didn't want him because I didn't want to be a part of his fan club. Deep down inside, I wanted all of him and my pussy knew it too. She wanted it just as well with her thirsty ass dripping wet like that.

"Moe, what the hell are you doing here, and how the hell you know where I live?" I said this by finally lowering the gun but still keeping it in my hand because any sudden movement I will have to end this fine masterpiece standing in front of me.

"I don't like to discuss certain things over the phone. Plus, you stopped answering my calls after you assumed I was only at you to get at ole boy which is not the case, so I'm here to prove myself." He was looking at me dead in my eyes, and I couldn't help but be taken into his hypnotizing gaze.

"Okay, I'm listening. What do you have to say?" I went to take a seat next to him so he can tell me what was going on. "Wait a minute. Pause, how the hell you know where I stay Moe?"

"Miss Lady how many times do I have to tell you I got my resources and I find out any and everything I need to know about anything and anyone that catches my interest."

I couldn't do nothing but sit there and look at him dumbfounded. I mean, damn he is the man of these streets. Hell, he even got some of the pigs on his payroll. We sat on the porch while he told me about him and Loco's interactions and their beef between one another and how when we meet he didn't know that I had dealings with Loco till he came over to the crib that day to drop off my car. And even then, he was still only interested in me and not me being associated with him. Besides, he knew our dealings together were over from me putting Loco out and closing the door in his face so he wasn't concerned.

I informed him what had went on between me and Loco to make us split up and that Cinnamon had just had the twins by him. I had also informed him that I had just found out I was pregnant and it was indeed Loco's baby. He agreed due to that nature and him becoming a new father that he would bury the beef with him out of respect for me and let them continue to set up shop since he had to make a living for his kids. Right then and there, I had gained more respect for this nigga and became more interested in him. Just on the strength of me, The Biggest King Pin in Tha G will let a nigga live to raise his kids. On top of all that, he didn't mind that I was carrying this nigga's baby. He still wanted me and I damn sure wanted him.

As soon as I offered for him to come in, his phone rings telling him that The Link Bar has burned to the ground. He asked me to ride with him, and I'm praying all the way there that this had nothing to do with Loco. Deep down inside, I knew that this had Loco's name written all over it. Especially, due to the fact that he feels Moe set him up to go to jail, which reminded me that I didn't even ask Moe about that. It will have to wait another day. On the drive there, the car was quiet as hell. Shit, you can hear a pin drop in that mug. I glanced over at Moe, and he looked so mad that his eyes were bloodshot red and you could see the steam coming from his nostrils.

Just by looking at him, I was scared to even turn the radio on to get the awkward silence out of the car, but considering we had at least another 25 more minutes to go, I took my chances and turned it on anyway. He had the CD by Desiigner in and my song "Panda" blazed through the speakers:

Panda, Panda Panda, Panda, Panda, Panda, Panda

I got broads in Atlanta

Twisting dope, lean, and the Fanta,

Credit cards and scammers,

I was bobbing my head, dancing, and singing along with the music. I saw Moe look at me out the corner of his eye and smile. Damn, this nigga had the most beautiful smile ever, showing all his purely white teeth.

"So you like this song, huh, shorty. You all into this shit." he said to me laughing, and I couldn't do nothing but laugh right along with him, because I have to admit I was feeling it. By the time we pulled up to the club, all of his workers and right-hand men were on the scene and so was the neighborhood. Netta had text me and told me she was there so when I got out the car, she was the first person I saw. I wasn't expecting to see Loco there at all, and when we locked eyes, I gave him a nod to let him know everything was cool, but for some odd strange reason that wasn't good enough.

Loco started walking towards us, and I knew that Moe was ready to go to war if he had to by the way he tensed up while holding my hand. Then Moe got another call stating that the strip club had also went up in flames. I walked dead in front of Moe so they couldn't get too close to one another. I didn't even pay attention to Moe's men surrounding us both and they all up choppers at the same time including Loco and his crew. All I heard was Loco say, "Asha and Netta, it's time for y'all to go."

I mean, for real though. Right in front of the laws and a crowd of people they had no chill. Good thing one twelve was all into the crime scene and didn't pay attention. I pleaded with Loco to leave before he went to jail, and if he cared anything about me or this baby he would leave. He looked at me and started to bag back. Moe instructed his men to retreat back as well. This was not the time or the place he said. We continued to head towards the building, and from what I can see, there was nothing left but the frame. The building was completely gone along with everything in it.

Moe just sat there and looked while he talked to the detectives. He informed them that he had to get to his other spot that ha also went up in flames as well. The detective gave him his card and told him to come down to the station later on once he was done. We left that scene and went straight to the strip club. There was no difference in this scene. Everything was gone and completely burned to the ground.

I felt so bad for Moe, because he looked real upset and hurt over the situation. Granted, he wouldn't be hurting for shit. Hell, he owned damn near the whole city. But the two clubs that burnt down was his money makers. Leave it to me to be as horny as I was and as fine as this nigga was looking, I was willing to do whatever I needed to do to relieve all his stress, tension, and problems. Hell, mind you, the last time I fucked was three months ago when I got knocked up by Loco, and shit, Moe was even sexier mad. My little pregnant pussy was pulsating and throbbing just by looking at him, and tonight, she was bound to get all of him.

Once we got in the car, I asked him if he was okay. He looked at me and smiled and told me not to worry my pretty little head. He rubbed the side of my face and gave me a peck on the forehead. That alone gave me chills, and I couldn't wait for this nigga to pull off because he was about to have the time of his life. I was finally willing to give into this nigga regardless of the circumstances. I can no longer hold back. I needed to nut and get my pussy fucked bad, and I wanted to see what this fine motherfucker was working with, so it was on like Ray Don Chong.

We pulled off and I popped in the throwback CD he had in his CD case, because I noticed my song R. Kelly "You Remind Me" on it, and that was the perfect song to get to work.

You remind me of my jeep, I wanna ride it

Something like my sound, I wanna pump it

Girl you look just like my cars, I wanna wax it

As soon as it started blazing through the speakers, I started massaging his manhood while he was driving. All he can do was moan and try to stay focused on the road. I felt his bulge grow through his jeans, so I unzipped his pants and his anaconda popped outstanding at full attention. Damn that was a beautiful sight to see. All twelve inches along with his mushroom shaped head just made my love potion a waterfall. I got my mouth watery as hell and let a trickle of my saliva fall down on his penis as I stroked him in a circular motion with my hand. Seeing his veins bulging out his dick and hearing his moans made me wetter every time he got louder. I instantly took his whole manhood in my mouth.

As I slob and bob all over his dick, I made sure to move my hand in a rapidly circular motion and twirled my tongue around the tip of his head while massaging his balls all at the same time, which drove him insane. All you heard was me slurping and him moaning and groaning.

"Damn Asha, baby. You gone make us crash. Awe shit, girl. Damn, right their baby. Bay… oohh, Asha don't stop."

Before I knew it, we were back at my house in no time. I think that nigga did like 100 MPH on the highway. He jumped out the car and came to my side opening the door, picked me up, and rushed me into the house.

As soon as we walked in, we barely made it through the front door. We were ripping each other's clothes off. This man was so muscular and strong he lifted me all the way up in the air and positioned me on his face while his tongue made my sexcapade an ice skating rink. He flicked his tongue around my clit while fingering me in my ass and holding me in the air all at the same time. I couldn't help myself; I was screaming with pleasure from the top of my lungs. If I stayed in an apartment, they would have called the police by now and swore the boy was killing me.

He laid me gently on the couch and had my legs pinned back. Shoot you would have never thought a pregnant chick would be this flexible. Hell, I didn't know my legs can go back that far myself.

He looked at me so seductively and said, "You sure you want this, because once I enter, ain't no turning back, and this pussy right here gone be mines for good, and it's gone belong to me, so are you sure you can handle that?"

All I can do was shake my head and not even a moment later, he was knocking my back out. This nigga was fucking me so good I didn't know whether I should scream, run, push him back or what all I can do was try to take every single inch he gave me.

Now don't get me wrong. Loco's dick was big too, and he knew how to work it, but this nigga Moe had me on a whole different level. Shit, Loco didn't have shit on him. I felt like I was on a different planet the way this nigga was making me feel oh so good. My pussy was gripping onto his dick for dear life like she never wanted to let it go. My eyes were rolled in the back of my head and I was clawing at his back, arms, and pushing him back all at the same damn time. Shit, this nigga was working with a monster, and I couldn't figure out what to do, so he made my mind up for me.

This nigga took my hands and held them back with my ankles and went to work. All I heard him say was, "Didn't I tell you to take it? It wasn't no turning back. I told you to move your hands. This my pussy right?"

I moaned so loud it echoed throughout the house, "Ooohhh shit, yes Daddy, yes, yes, yes! It's yours! It's all yours. Ooh, Moe. Awe shit, baby. I'm coming, I'm coming."

And just like that, I exploded all over his steel rod. He flipped me over and said, "I'm not done yet." I thought to myself, *this nigga finna tear my insides up all night.*

Chapter 13- Accomplished

Moe

Man, waking up the next morning to the sight of Asha lying next to me was something I have been trying to accomplish for a while now. My goal was to make Miss Asha my lady by any means necessary as soon as I laid eyes on her. It didn't make it no better when she tried to play hard to get. That only made me want her even more, and I'm the type of nigga that, if I want it, I'm going to get. I don't take no for an answer, so she was as good as got. Oh, and by the way I'm Moe, which is short for Monroe King. I'm known as the man of these streets which I'm sure you probably have heard about me already, but anyway, I'm not your typical King Pin as they say.

You see, I was born and raised in Chicago, IL. Some may call it Chi-Town or Chiraq, but either way, those are my stomping grounds. Me and my family moved to Gary, IN when I was like ten years old. My mom thought it was better than being in the windy city. Yea right. Hell, Scary Gary is just like a miniature Chicago if you asked me. By the time I was fourteen, I got hooked in with the wrong crowd, and they easily turned me on to the dope gang and the street life. I fell victim to that fast money really quick not really knowing what the hell I was getting myself into, but shit, I wasn't no dumb ass nigga. I caught on really quick.

Now, a nigga was smart as hell. You know, I was making that honor roll shit, you feel me, so I had the brains and all. I made sure I did my research before I went full fledge as an all-out dope boy, so I knew the risk and some I wasn't willing to take. I was a mathematician and really good with numbers so I had that advantage over the old heads that been in the game for a while. I was also good with managing money and new how to invest in shit to make more.

I always wanted to be my own boss. Never liked taking orders or directions from a motherfucker, so once I was done with high school, I planned on getting some degrees in business, and that's exactly what I did. Yea, like I said, I wasn't your average D-Boy. By the time I took over these Gary streets, I had a Master's in

Business Management and Administration, and I had already owned *Scores* the strip club which had just burned down.

Yea I was only 19 when I got my first business and was only in my first year of college. I was already in the process of taking over the streets right from up under the niggas who put me on, and they didn't even realize it because I stayed behind the scene. See, when the Five-O look at me, they see a regular business man that's black, and that's all. Yea, I'm known in the streets but in the professional industry, I'm referred to as Mr. King or Monroe King.

I was also stereotyped as the street nigga that was too pretty to get my hands dirty. Yea right; if they only knew that that was one of my turn-ons… to beat a nigga ass and see his ass leaking somewhere. Now, I've been told that I favor some model named Chadoy Leon whoever the fuck that is, but they say we look like twins. The only difference is I got braids and this nigga don't. Funny thing is I never took the time out to see if I look like this nigga or not. Hell, I didn't care because it didn't contain my paper so it wasn't containing me. Anyway niggas hated on me all the time for that shit because I had the ladies wrapped around my pinky finger.

They were willing to do whatever just to get at me just for my looks alone, and to add money, fame, and being the man to it made it an extra bonus to them. Everybody wanted to be Mrs. King but I wasn't on it till now. I never thought about settling down with a female. Hell, I never been in a relationship with one. Females just threw themselves at me willingly regardless if they had a man or not. Shit, I done had hoes leave their husbands just to get in on the action so how do you wife that? Shit I wasn't going. Now, don't get me wrong, back in the day, I was sweet on this one little shorty I grew up with named Lacey.

Lacey lived right next door to us when we moved to Gary, and we became real close instantly. She was mixed with black and white, hair was down to her ass, and she was thick as hell. She kind of reminded you of Lauren London if you asked me. Just thinking about her puts a smile on my face. See, Lacey was a good girl and wasn't about that street life, and she couldn't handle the, as I called them, fans that came along with it, so we stayed into it all the time and a nigga like me don't like to argue, this was one of the reasons why our relationship was on and off.

Lacey wanted a nigga all to herself and wanted me to leave the street life along. Now I can completely understand why, but that wasn't in my plans no time soon. I still had shit I needed to accomplish. She was the type to give a nigga an ultimatum of either her or the streets. Now, I loved Lacey, true enough, but I wasn't that in love like she was. She was never willing to fully leave me alone since I'm the only dude she ever fucked with. Like literally I'm her first everything. I remember it like it was yesterday when I popped that cherry wide open and she been sprung ever since.

I can admit that it's been times where I did think about settling down with Lacey and marrying her. Hell, she has been by a nigga side since we were shorties, but damn, if anything was to ever happen to me, she would let my whole empire go to waste, and I worked too hard to get to where I am to let that happen. See, I needed a down ass chick that was about that life and wouldn't think twice about taking over if need be, and then I meet Asha. She was everything I was looking for in a woman. Umm, umm, umm, baby girl had it going on. Now, I don't know about everyone else, but to me Asha reminded me of a thick ass Nia Long, and when I say thick, I mean thick from ass and titties to thighs, and a banging ass body.

That's not the only thing that attracted me to Asha though. I love the way she carried herself; she had that attitude and confidence within herself where she knew she was the shit and ain't nobody gone stop her show. That right there alone in a female is sexy as shit to hold your head up high and don't let nothing or no one stand in your way. Yea, that right there is Asha. Not only that, but she was about that street life, got an education, can hold her own, plus she was the only female, naw scratch that, the only person that ever told me no and really made me work for what I wanted. Having her tell me no made me infatuated with her ass, and I wanted her ten times more. By any means, I was going to get her.

I don't know why but that playing hard to get shit turned a nigga on in ways I didn't even know existed. Yea, she had me hooked around her pinky finger and didn't even know it. I was willing to give it all up for her so right then and there I knew she would be the Mrs. As far as her shorty goes, I was willing to step in and take care of him or her like it was my own. Asha started moving in her sleep which distracted me from my thoughts, and I knew she was bound to wake up soon so I decided that breakfast in bed would suit her. I got up to cook breakfast, and I was thinking that some bacon, eggs, and French toast would do.

So what, I bet y'all thought a nigga can't cook. Shit, my Chef Boyardee skills were off the chain. Just call me Chef King. After making breakfast, I went to wake up Asha in the most pleasing way. She was still laying there looking so delicious, and I had all access to her treasure spot. I sat both plates down on the nightstand, kissed her on her little baby bump, and spread her lips to get a better look at her pretty little pink pussy. Soon as I got to flicking my tongue across her clit, she got to moaning and spreading her legs further apart giving me full access. She arched her back up and grabbed a hold to the back of my head pulling my braids and let all of her love juices come pouring out.

"Good morning beautiful. Here is your breakfast. You have to feed the little one. Then get dressed; we got runs to make."

She looked at me and smiled then said, "Oh damn, Moe you cooked this? You didn't tell me you can cook. Thanks bae."

After breakfast, Asha washed the dishes while I took a phone call about some drops that needed to be handled and money that needed to be picked up. It was business as usual like any other day. I made a note to contact my connect back in Mexico because it was almost time to re-up. Walking back into the house, Asha was already in the bathroom getting the shower ready.

Standing there looking at her, I felt so complete. Not to mention she looked like a masterpiece of art waiting to be displayed. Her pregnancy glow didn't make things no better and it didn't give my mans a chance. He was already standing at attention. Asha didn't notice me standing there so I simply got undressed and picked her up to get in the shower. All she could do is giggle. I kissed her gently on her soft lips and she parted them accepting my tongue willingly. She took my mans and inserted him into her love spot,

"AWE SHIT, MOE," was all she could say as I started to slide her all the way down on this big ass dick.

Feeling her walls wrap around my dick tighter and tighter as I pushed deeper into her had me going crazy. I picked up the pace and she immediately started clawing at my back, "Uuugh Asha baby, that's my pussy?" I knew it was mine from the first encounter by the way she screamed and gripped me as she was taking the dick, but I like hearing her tell me it's mines.

"OOH SHIT! OOH SHIT! YES, MOE! IT'S YOURS! IT'S ALL YOURS! DAMN BAE." Hearing her tell me that made me go full force and start drilling the shit out her pussy.

"You love this big ass dick, don't you?"

I felt her pussy start throbbing around my dick and she instantly threw her head back. Her eyes rolled in the back of her head, and I knew right then and there she was about to come.

"Yes, baby. I love this dick. Awe shit, Moe. I love you bae. Ooooh, shit." she said as she climaxed all over my huge rod of steel, and I came right along with her. After getting my rocks off, we had to take a cold shower, because the water was now cold. We got out the shower, and I smacked her on her ass. I told her to hurry up and get dressed; we were running late. She obliged and went to do just that, when my phone rings, and what do you know, it's Lacey.

Chapter 14- Game Plan

Loco

Man, I was so pissed off to see Asha with this bitch ass nigga after everything we told her about the nigga. I was so ready to put a hot one in his ass right then and there. Hell, I didn't even care about One Time being at the crime scene. That nigga lucky Asha was there and saved his motherfucking life, cause if it wasn't for her stepping in the middle of it and telling me to calm down, it was gone be one. The one thing I can't get over though is Asha knows what the hell the deal is yet she still around this dude, so I'm going to need to see what's going on with that. That shit is putting her and my seed in jeopardy.

Since Asha has an OBGYN appointment tomorrow, we can discuss it then. Today, it's all about my twins though. I have to say it felt good having my family over to the house along with Cinnamon's peoples. I was in a happy, comfortable place, and it made me think about actually settling down with Cinnamon. I mean, damn shorty has been after a nigga for a minute and don't even care that my heart is still with another chick. She still trying to win me over, but the thing with that is I need a girl with some self-esteem about themselves, and with Cinnamon, she didn't give a damn what I did as long as she can claim me as hers, and that was a turn off for me.

Dancing with my mom to our favorite old school joint brought back a lot of memories. I just so happen to look up and notice Cinnamon watching us just smiling. A feeling came over me and I thought maybe this can work. She was looking gorgeous, and not to mention, she did pick up a lil weight from the twins, but it was all in the right places. Damn, just thinking about that, I couldn't wait to be up in that shit again. She needs to hurry up and heal from that C-section. Just then, I got a text message that took me straight out of my thoughts.

The message was from a shorty I met around the way named Lacey. Now, Lacey was this bad ass redbone that I was trying to smash but shorty said she had a dude, which frankly, I didn't give a fuck. Of course, a nigga got to play his cards right, so we decided to just be friends. Yea, lil mama was playing right into my hands; we were gone be friends alright… friends with benefits if I played this shit right. She was upset saying her and her dude was into it and she needed someone to talk to.

Hell, tonight just might be the night, so I text her back telling her to meet me at Dave and Busters over in Orlando Park about 8:30. She agreed stating that it might just be what she needed to take her mind away from everything. *Yea, if I ever get a hold to that, I'm turning her the fuck out,* I thought. I looked up when I heard the twins crying and Cinnamon was trying to tend to them, so I decided to help her feed them. I have to say I loved the hell out of my babies and loved that I was a father even though I didn't want to be one at first.

After getting the twins settled back down, I had the D.J. play a slow song so I can dance with Cinnamon. I didn't want her to feel like I was ignoring her at all. You know females get that postpartum depression and shit, and I couldn't deal with that. I had them to take it all the way back to and play Color Me Badd's "I Want to Sex You Up":

I wanna sex you up.

All night.

You make me feel real good.

I wanna rub you down.

Yea that's right. I went way way back. Everyone got up and got to dancing to that shit, and that was the perfect song because that is exactly what I wanted to do and believe me, she knew it. She wanted it just as bad as I did; maybe even more.

After dancing with Cinnamon, Nate called my phone to give me an update on this nigga Moe. He told me that Asha, Autumn, that nigga Weed, and Moe's hoe ass was seen out there in *River Oaks* mall doing a damn shopping spree buying baby shit. *What the fuck this nigga thinks he doing splurging on my shorty?* Yea, I couldn't help but laugh because I knew with Asha fucking around with this nigga I can easily get to him and have Asha set his ass up for me, so I told Nate this just might be a benefit for us and to let them continue to do them but keep the trail on him.

After eating and opening up gifts, me and Cinnamon took all the twins gifts and things into the house and helped my mom clean up. Even after everyone took plates home, we still had enough food to feed the block, so I called my crew over to get some food for their family. I told Cinnamon that I had some shit to take care of so I jumped in the shower to get ready to meet Lacey. I decided to throw on my Ferrari King Gold watch, with my Turkfit outfit I bought the other day, my gold chain to match my watch, and my Jay's. I topped it off with my 3 am Sean John cologne. Yea, I was looking good.

"Well, you look nice to be going to just handle some business." Cinnamon said. I think she kind of had a feeling I was up to no good but oh well. I just kissed her on her cheek and walked out. I got to Dave and Busters by 8:25 and what do you know Lacey was already there looking astonishing. We decided to go and take our seat to eat first before playing any of the games.

I asked her what was she so upset about and she preceded to tell me that her and her dude have been on shaky terms, and she thinks that they will end up splitting for good. *Oh yea, jack pot,* I thought to myself. It's time to wheel her on in.

"So why do you think y'all gone split for good when you said it's normal for y'all to break up and get back together. Haven't y'all been down this road before?" I was asking Hella question to get all the information I needed to make her my next victim to this long ass snake of mines.

"Yea, we usually do, but it has never been the way it is now. See, he has been real distant towards me lately, and I believe he has a baby on the way."

I noticed a tear fall from her face when she said that so being the gentleman I am, I gently wiped the tear from her face, kissed her on the check, and told her to smile and that everything will be alright.

Seeing the hurt in her made me realize tonight wasn't the night, and I just felt like getting her mind off of what she was going through. I did notice that she was falling for me, and I knew it will happen soon, so I decided to be patient. For the remainder of the night, we played the games and I let her beat me in a few of the basketball tournaments to make her feel good. She really thought she was winning too. I made sure she walked away with the biggest teddy bear in there, and I sprayed it with my cologne, so she cuddles up with it tonight and think it was me there with her.

The next day, I met up with Asha at Dr. Brown's office to get her 4-month checkup for the baby. We learned she was having a boy so we decided to name him Lorenzo Jones Jr. Even though he not the first boy, I still wanted a Jr and Cinnamon wanted the twins' names to sound alike and I was cool with that. I was happy that me and Asha was finally able to be civil with one another and talk about things. She even thanked me for stepping up and taking responsibility for the baby. We agreed to have lunch together after the appointment to finish talking about our co-parenting between one another.

We met up at Lincoln's by 5th Ave and ordered some US Steele sandwiches, something Asha has been craving for lately. I asked her if she was thinking about being involved with Moe even though she knew what was going on.

"Loco, who I'm with and involved with is none of your concern. All you should be concerned about is your son."

"Damn Asha, for real though. You know you got my heart girl, and you know I got beef with this nigga, so that is my concern, because I don't want you or my baby caught in the crossfire." As soon as I said that, she looked at me and started wrapping up here food. "Wait Asha, don't leave. You know I want you, and I love you, so why are you acting like that? On top of that, I don't want you with no one else and you know that so stop flexin' boo."

She just sat there, looked at me, and shook her head. Then she said, "Loco, I can't do this with you anymore. You hurt me to my core, and if you loved me so much, you would have never broken my heart and had kids with another woman."

And just like that, she walked out leaving me sitting there stuck. I can't be mad though, because she was right, and I did hurt her. Her heart was damaged completely, so I knew there was no turning back for her.

Chapter 15- The Rush

Cinnamon

So Loco got up this morning to meet Asha at the doctor for her 4-month checkup. Yea this nigga got me fucked in the game. This baby will never make it to see the light of day and his so-called love of his life ain't about to make it either. Hell, this bitch barely came to my doctor's appointment, but want to be front and center for hers. Naw, I ain't going. It ends today, so as soon as he left, I called my sister Nina and asked her to come over to watch the twins while I make a run. I knew exactly where Asha's doctor's office was so I went there and waited for them to come out.

I decided to follow this bitch and catch her slipping. It was going to be an easy task because I copped another whip so no one will know it was me. Especially not driving a bucket; it was below my standards. I saw Asha and Loco come out of the doctor's office all cheesy and shit like they were the happiest couple ever. That shit made my blood boil, and it took everything in me not to get out the car and beat her ass right then and there.

Upon leaving out of the parking lot, I noticed her and Loco going in the same direction. Now, what the fuck is this shit when this nigga is supposed to bring his ass straight home. "Really Loco? Yeah, I see I'm about to go ham on his ass too. This nigga just really took this bitch on a date to some damn Lincolns. Okay we're going to see about this." Sitting there in the parking lot, I'm watching them and she looks a little too comfy with my man.

Asha finally gets up to leave and here he goes trying to make her stay. I guess he thought I was playing, and he must take me for a joke when I told him if I can't have him after all this no one can. She finally leaves and Loco sits there for a while; I follow Asha as she heads to the highway. I didn't want things to be suspicious so I called Loco.

"Hey bay, is you still at the doctors?"

"Naw, I'm on my way home. Be there in about a half an hour. Why, what's up?"

"Nothing, just missing you, that's all. I will see you when you get home."

And just like that, we ended the call and I started my attack. The highway was pretty clear so that was a good thing. It wouldn't be no witnesses. My windows were tinted so you couldn't make out a driver. I started to do at least 90 MPH to catch up with her since I let her get some distance on me.

And WHAM, there you go. I ran that hoe off the road and her car flipped like three times. I laughed and went on about my way. I was confident that there was no surviving that. After I drove for about three miles down the road, I heard all types of sirens from police, ambulance, and fire trucks. Well, the bitch done learned today that I'm not to be fucked with.

I called up my connect to come and get rid of the car once I got home. I got a call from Loco saying he was on his way to the hospital because Asha was in a car accident. Of course that pissed me off, but hey, it was expected, and I had to play my cards right so he wouldn't be suspicious. I just said okay and told him to keep me posted. I let my sister Nina out of the house and locked up, went into the living room to watch TV. They had the whole entire accident scene on the news.

All you see is pregnant woman car flips three times on highway 80/94. What pissed me off is it wasn't giving an update to let me know if she was dead or alive. Oh well, I guess I will have to get that information from Loco. I went to check on the twins and get them ready to take a bath for bed. They were still fast asleep so I made their bottles and got out their sleepers and made their bath water.

As soon as I went to get one of the twins, I get a call from Loco.

"Hey bae is everything okay?" I asked him as soon as I answered the phone.

"Yea man, she cool. Just a little banged up and she started having contractions so they gave her some medicine to stop them. Other than that it's a waiting game."

I couldn't believe what I was hearing. *This bitch is still alive. Ugh, why don't she fucking get lost already? She is ruining my damn life* I thought to myself.

"So she is alive and so is the baby?"

"Yea man, Junior cool. He seems like he ready to come up out of their though, but Asha had on her seatbelt so they said she might have a concussion. They gone keep her of course for observation and their monitoring the baby. Her contractions slowed down a little; hopefully the medicine works to stop them completely."

I couldn't do nothing but roll my eyes and think of another plan to terminate this hoe once and for all. Till then, I had to act like a little concerned, supporting girlfriend.

"So I hear you say Junior. Do that means it's a boy?"

"Oh shit, yea bae. I'm sorry. We didn't get a chance to talk about what went on at the doctors huh, but she having a boy and we're naming him Lorenzo Jones Jr." I laughed so hard when he said that it was funny since he wasn't the first boy. "What the hell so funny Cinnamon?"

"The fact that he is a junior and not the first boy."

I guess me saying that and laughing must of pissed him off because he hung up on me. Oh well, he will get over it. After Loco hung the phone up on me, I attended to my precious babies and gave them their bath and fed them for the night. Now all that was left to do is call my connect to come up with another plan.

"Hey D-Bo, we need to go back to the drawing board, because the bitch and that baby still alive."

"Well damn, Cinnamon. How the fuck did she survive that shit. I seen it on the news and that car is fucked?"

"I know right. Same thing I said, but according to Loco she had on a seatbelt and she went into labor but they are stopping her contractions." After saying that, the phone got real quiet. "Hello D-Bo, are you there?"

"Yea man, I'm here. I was just thinking do you know where this girl live?"

"Naw I don't know where she lives but I'm sure it's not hard to find out. All we gotta do is put a trail on her. Why you ask?"

"Because shit since that shit ain't work I'm thinking since you said shorty do got money our payout could be a home invasion on her gone wrong. Instead of you coming out your pockets, we can kill two birds with one stone."

Hearing the sound of that sounded really good, "You know what, that sounds like a plan. I will hit you up as soon as I know she will be released from the hospital."

And just like that, a plan was in place, and I couldn't have been more satisfied in knowing that Asha was about to be the last of my problems.

Chapter 16- Payback

Lacey

I can't believe Moe will sit up here and play me like that in front of another bitch. The nerve of him after all we been through, and as long as I been by his side through all his bullshit. Okay, it's cool. I got his ass. Payback's a bitch, and this nigga acts like I can't go out and be with another man. But it's okay for him to be with all these hoes. Cool okay, now watch me work. What makes it so bad is that this hoe pregnant, and I know damn well he didn't get a girl pregnant on me with all the many abortions he made me get when I was pregnant by him.

Oh, and by the way, I'm Lacey Rae. I'm the girl who Moe is in a relationship with and has been since we were little. As you can see, I'm his go-to chick and his ride or die chick. You see I been there through everything and when I say everything, I mean everything with this man. I done been around for a minute and fought more chicken heads than a little bit. Hell, it's been a few times I done even fought Moe for trying to play me with all these females he attracts. Now, I know with his reputation it comes with the territory. Hell, he is the King Pin of the streets and got money out his ass.

But the thing is I been with this man before he had all of that. Hell, he was flat broke, and I was still there, so it ain't about the money with me. I really truly love him with everything in me, but it's time to show him that he can no longer walk all over me, and I'm just going to allow it. It's time for me to move on which I'm sure will make him shape up, so I met this dude by the name of Loco a few weeks ago.

Now Loco is fine as hell; he reminds me of a knock-off version of old boy that plays on "Hit The Floor", McKinley Freeman also known as Derek Roman on the show. Yea he had him down to the tee. The difference was Loco got some hazel brown sexy eyes and his body was full of tats. That nigga got it going on. Not to mention he is working with a monster. Now, I haven't fucked the nigga or nothing, but damn, you couldn't help but notice that big ass dick print in his pants. Hell, his shit hangs down to his fucking knees. I don't see how it even fits in his pants.

Oh goodness I can just imagine the extent his dick gets when it's hard. Umm, umm, umm. Okay Lacey; let's snap it back to reality here because thinking about him got me soaking up my damn thong and shit. Anyway, I met Loco down in DHB at the white store right off of Ridge Rd and Georgia St. I went in to get me a Pepsi and some chips. He was there buying him some blunts when I walked in and I immediately got his attention.

Now see I been told that I look like a mixed version of Lauren London since I'm mixed with black and white. I'm about 5'5 and I weigh about 145 lbs. My hair is down to my butt, I have green eyes, and a banging body. I wasn't stuck up or nothing like that but I have to give it to myself; I'm a fine ass chick. When Loco saw me, he immediately tried to holler. I was skeptical at first and wasn't on that due to fucking around with Moe. It was been times Moe done beat the shit out of dudes who approached me and whooped my ass as well because he says I shouldn't have given them something to look at. Huh, yea. This nigga is a trip, and like I said earlier, he wanted me all to himself, but everyone who wanted him had him.

On this particular day, it was something about this Loco that made me take the risk and give him my number. It was like the feeling of being scared of Moe's' reaction was no longer there anymore. Granted, it did take a while for me to call him so I would only text. It was easy enough to get rid of evidence and avoid an ass whooping. I bet you're thinking why am I letting Moe control my life and why am I so scared of him huh?

Well, to be honest, that is Moe for you. He is very controlling, and he is the type of man that will put you in the dirt if you cross him. Something I wasn't prepared for at the moment. I loved my life. I believed that man the last time he told me he will kill me if I ever gave his pussy to another man. After he beat me senseless for going out on a date when we were broken up. Sitting here thinking about all this shit makes me wonder how and why I put up with it for so long. I guess it's because Moe is my first everything, and when I say everything, I mean everything. This man took my virginity, was my first kiss, boyfriend, love… everything. Truth be told he has been my only boyfriend.

After seeing what I saw the other day at *River Oaks* mall, it made a bitch grow some big balls. I wanted Moe to hurt and hurt bad just the way he had hurt me, and I didn't care what it took to do it. Let me explain my reasons for having a change of heart. Me and Moe have a house together out in Lansing, IL. Now don't get me wrong, this man has multiple houses, and maybe it's safe to say I have a house in Lansing because really that's what it was. Moe was only there from time to time when we were on good terms or he will stop through when he wanted to get his dick wet.

Besides all that, he paid all the bills and he do have some belongings there so I say our house. Well, earlier that day, Moe left me some money to go shopping with like he does every week, nothing out of the ordinary. The difference is, I usually don't shop with it. I add it to my bank account that he is unaware of for a rainy day. Today, I was feeling a little down because Moe had started to ignore me and was giving me the cold shoulder. Every phone call I made he sent me straight to voicemail and every text I sent went unanswered.

A shopping spree was what I needed to clear my head and to get myself out of this funk I was in. And what do you know, I get to the mall and I'm coming out of Victoria's Secret from buying me some new undies and lingerie for this nigga and he up in there with a whole brand new bitch. Like I said earlier, I'm used to beating a bitch down over Moe, and yea, I'm used to seeing him cheat and be with other hoes but this time was different. I acted a whole ass in the mall because this bitch was pregnant and he out splurging buying baby items and shit. Just remembering this whole scene and letting it play out in my head over and over again makes my blood boil. I'm sure my blood pressure is through the roof right about now.

To make a long story short, I walked up to Moe and his side piece and went off immediately. Now Moe usually just sit there and laugh at me and will let me and the girl go at it without interfering. I think that type of shit turned him on to see females fight over him, but this day he was ready to fight me.

As soon as I said, "Moe, what the fuck is this shit? So this why you're ignoring my calls and text? You're with this bitch out here splurging and shit, and I know this hoe ain't pregnant?" before I knew it, Moe had me pinned up to the wall by my neck choking the shit out of me and then gone tell me,

"Look here bitch; this ain't got nothing to do with you so I advise you to watch your mouth and go head on somewhere. You disrespect her again and I will snap your fucking neck."

When I say that shit hurt, that shit hurt. He just confirmed to me that I didn't mean shit to him out of all this time. He never took another bitch's side, and I knew right then and there that it was his baby she was carrying. That broke me down to the core; it wasn't no coming back from that. How can he create a life with someone else and I'm supposed to be okay with it? Homeboy got another thang coming. After that day, I couldn't stop crying. I seriously wanted to kill Moe's ass, but I knew I would never get away with it, so I settled for the next best thing that he wouldn't tolerate.

Now mind you, I said earlier that I had multiple abortions by Moe. He has always told me he wasn't ready for kids and the lifestyle he lives bringing a child in the world wouldn't be smart. He didn't want to give these niggas a reason to come after his family or leave his child fatherless. I really understood that. Even though I wanted to be a mother, I never wanted to raise a baby on my own if anything was to ever happen to him, so I always agreed to the abortion. And even if I didn't, he would probably beat the baby out of me.

The first time I got pregnant by Moe, I was 15 and still in high school. I was scared shitless. Moe was just now coming up in the drug world and still learning some of the ropes. Considering we both were still in high school, neither one of us was fit to have a baby. Especially living in my household. Hell, I wasn't fit to live in my dysfunctional house, so I damn sure didn't want a baby living there. We never told our parents about the pregnancy. We just went to Chicago and had the procedure done. It was a little low, low place to where we didn't need our parents' consent.

Hum, this shit is crazy. Now that I think about it, I done had a total of six abortions by this man and one miscarriage that I just had recently, only a month ago. Now he has the nerve to have another bitch carrying his seed. My heart was completely broken and this time there was no way I can forgive him for this, so I decided to get REVENGE for breaking my heart and call up Loco. It's time I test the waters and see what life has to offer.

Chapter 17- Grateful

Asha

So, I finally decided to give Moe a chance out of all this time and boy I tell you this man is amazing. He has been a complete gentleman and has been catering to me since I let him spend the night with me. Ohh, Jesus. Speaking of letting him spend the night, my oh my, that man turned me all the way out something serious. When I say he laid the pipe down, baby he laid it down. Had a sister walking different and shit, and my pussy was sore as fuck. Shit come to think about it, on the low, I think I'm sprung off his dick. Hell, Loco never sexed me as good as Moe did.

It's just something about Moe's sex game that got me in my feelings. I don't know if it's the pregnancy talking or because this is the first time I done had sex in months. And maybe just maybe his shit the real deal but this nigga had me screaming like it was no tomorrow. Knocking my back out was a complete understatement for what he did that night. Hell words can't explain it. Not only is the dick good but his head game is on ten. That shit so good I couldn't take it. This nigga had me running from the tongue. It was like he knew my body better than I did, hell, better than Loco did and Loco knew my body well.

The way we were going at it that night you would have thought we were making a porno starring Asha and Moe. Truth be told, considering where I live, I'm surprised the neighbors didn't call the police, because I was loud as hell, and I knew they heard me. After all that hot sex, I woke up to some more bomb as head and breakfast in bed. Now this some shit I can get used to. Having sex in the shower gave me the ultimate view of his sexy ass body and all his tattoos. I'm a sucker for a man with tats. That's a complete turn-on for me, and his body was full of them, not to mention, he had a sexy ass body with muscles and cuts in all the right places.

Damn, just thinking about him got me horny as hell and ready to hop right back on his dick and ride him like a roller coaster. I love the way he handles me and my body. Man, I feel like I just hit the jackpot being with him. And when he said this shit is his from now on, the brother wasn't lying. He trapped me as soon as his dick

entered my juice box. I'm really all his longs he keeps sexing me up

the way he did. Yea, I can completely understand how and why this

man had all these females feeling some type of way and going crazy

over him. Even though I was crazy for him and that monster he toting

around, I refused to fall victim to that bunch of females that acts

crazy over him. He will never know he hooked me like that.

Speaking of girls going crazy, let me tell you what happen

the next day. So Moe takes me on a shopping spree completely

unexpected. I mean the man said he had business to handle; I wasn't

expecting the business was shopping for me and my son. Anyway,

we go and pick up my cousin Autumn and of course she still messes

with Weed on the low, so he came along as well. We ended up at

River Oaks Mall and Moe tells me to have fun and that everything

was on him. Come on now. Y'all know me; I'm not the one to take

handouts from a nigga. I got my own paper and can splurge on

myself but this nigga insisted.

Needless to say, Weed came to splurge on Autumn too so between the both of us we went all out. Since I haven't done any baby shopping, I took this opportunity to do just that. I got baby clothes, a crib, a swing and any and everything a baby needed plus more. We spent a good ten stacks on baby items alone. As soon as I get to shopping for myself and my graduation which is next month, we run into one of Moe's fans.

Now this little half breed bitch came up to us talking crazy and out the side of her neck. Now you know with me and Autumn; this bitch would have had her teeth knocked down her throat, yet I'm pregnant so I couldn't do much at this point in time. And I really didn't have to. As soon as this girl got to calling me out my name, Autumn stepped forward to say something and never got the words out of her mouth. Moe grabbed this girl so quick and had her by her neck in the air going the fuck off. Baby girl looked so dumbfounded and walked out the mall without even saying another word.

I couldn't blame her though, because the look in this man's eyes had me scared to say something. He looked like the devil himself had took over him so we went on about our day like nothing ever happened. Autumn looked at me like bitch you gone question him about that. Shit I gave her that look back like hell naw, I'm good. I don't even need to know. Once we were done he ended up explaining to me who the girl was though and apologized for me seeing him in that way.

It turns out the girl's name was Lacey, someone who Moe had a relationship with back in the day. He said that they grew up together and she was having a hard time letting him go; that she didn't believe that it will never be a him and a her. She feels that because of their history she is destined to be his wife and won't take no for an answer. So he has to show her better than he can tell her. Listening to their history had me thinking that this has got to be the dumbest bitch in the United States of America.

Now I'm not a lesbian or anything, and I don't have nothing against them, but hell shorty was a bad chick. Hell, if I did swing that way, trust and believe I would be on shorty. She was just too damn pretty to be settling for a nigga that no longer wanted her, so I figured she must have had some self-esteem issues or something. She had to because I'm sure she can pull any nigga she wanted. Anyway, I did explain to Moe that I didn't like the fact that he put his hands on her and his response was,

"I don't give a fuck if it's male or female. Anyone who disrespects you can get it. You mine and I'm going to protect what belongs to me."

That right there let me know I was in over my head with him. After our little shopping spree, we went to drop off Autumn and Weed at Weed's house. Autumn claimed she needed to properly thank him for her gifts. Huh, we all know what that mean. Them two has been getting awfully close lately. I remember her calling me the first time she gave him a sample. She said she thinks he broke or busted something in her.

That was the funniest shit I have ever heard. My poor little cousin was ready to go to the hospital after fucking him. Weed called her an amateur after that night. He said that she couldn't hang and she was running from him.

Autumn just laughed and said, "You got damn right nigga. Hell, I'm a little skinny bitch. That shit went all the way in my chest. You were gone have to hold me down for me to take all that dick like that. Then this nigga saw I couldn't handle it and wanted to go deeper and harder. I was scared for my life."

Them two are some real life characters though; they be having me laughing so hard when they are around that I be ready to piss my pants. I really enjoyed them especially considering I haven't been around my cousin much since I moved, and as of right now, I was missing her company.

To make matters worse, right after the shopping spree, I ended up in the hospital the very next day, and I believe this Lacey bitch got something to do with it. Now, let me tell you about this incident. So, I meet Loco at the doctor's office right here on 35th and Broadway for my monthly checkup. I was happy to learn we were having a boy and was thankful that Loco was present. Now, I can say Moe wasn't too happy, but he has to learn that this is between me, Loco, and our child, which has nothing to do with him.

Anyway Loco asked if we can talk about co-parenting our son over lunch which I agreed to because I was starving and was craving a US Steele sandwich from Lincoln's. Plus, it's a convo we needed to have. When we left the doctor's office parking lot, I peeped this old busted beat down car leaving as well. Mind you, I never seen anyone get in or out of the car so I figured they walked out the building way before we did so I didn't pay it no mind. I went on about my way to Lincolns as usual. Now, I got halfway down Broadway, like to 25th and Broadway, and saw this same car one car away from Loco's car. Still, I thought maybe we're all just going the same direction. Hell, Gary so small you bound to end up in the same destination anyway.

So once we pull into Lincolns, this same car slows down but keeps going. Still, my dumb ass didn't think twice about it. I just brushed it off. Hell, the only person I know for a fact got beef with me is Cinnamon, and from what I know, she at home with the twins. Now, Loco is a different story. This man got Hella beef, and the most recent is with Moe, so I knew it wasn't that since I was with him at the time and Moe knew that. To make a long story short, I leave the restaurant and head home. Out of nowhere I see this same damn car behind me on the freeway. That's when my intuition kicked in so I called Moe quickly and asked him if he had someone following me.

And just as I thought he didn't, before I could say anything else, the bastard ran me off the road and made my car flip over three times. All I could do is pray for me and my baby and hope that we will be okay. Thank God we were; I heard Moe screaming and yelling through the phone but my phone went flying Lord knows where in the car, so he did a GPS trace on my phone and sent the police and ambulance. Funny thing is he beat the ambulance there and was front and center going off on the doctors, nurses, and all to hurry up. He was telling them I'm pregnant and to save me and the baby. He said that if we die, he was killing everybody in this bitch.

This man was going crazy; I guess in the middle of everything he called my cousin Autumn because her and the rest of the crew was there along with Moe's crew. My family was there and I have no clue who called Loco but he was there with Netta and his mom. I tell you I almost shitted bricks seeing both of the crews in one confined space together I thought all hell was about to break lose but to my surprise everyone was more worried and concerned about me and the baby's safety. They put their beef to the side. Even took turns on visiting me without it being a hassle. One will come in and check on me and when that one will leave, the other will follow suit.

I am very grateful that they respected me and my son enough not to act crazy in the hospital. I was also grateful that me and my son was alive. Granted, I went into labor because of the impact the crash had on me and my body, but the doctors were able to stop the contractions. They said that it was a good thing I had on my seatbelt because it could have been a tragedy if I didn't. Needless to say me and my son are okay. I am a little sore and banged up but that will heal in due time.

Chapter 18- Miami

Moe

I should have never answered the damn phone for Lacey ass, but I seriously got tired of this bitch calling my phone back to back. I had to literally turn my shit off and keep it off the whole time I was at Asha's house. As soon as I powered the bitch on, and we get out the shower, here she goes again blowing a nigga up. I mean, damn, a nigga was deep off in some pussy and this bitch be blowing it. She is really about to end up on the block list straight up.

A nigga didn't even get hello out good enough before she starts going in talking about "Why the fuck you haven't been answering my calls? It's been two whole days and you haven't been home and you keep sending me to voicemail."

Right then and there I had to check this bitch. She was getting a little too comfortable and beside herself. I don't know who she thought I was, or who she was for that matter. I instantly went in on that ass.

"Hey, hold the fuck up, bitch. Last I checked, I was a grown ass fucking man and didn't need to check in with no bitch for one. Two, I been home to my crib. I don't know what your simple stupid-minded ass don't understand. You ain't my bitch so move the fuck around and if you keep calling my phone like that trying to check me, I will be the last motherfucker you call."

After I got my point across, I ended the call, and she didn't bother to call back. I proceeded to enjoy my time with Asha.

I took Asha on a shopping spree and we let my nigga and her cousin tag along. And guess what, we run smack dead into this bitch; it's like it's no fucking escaping her. Even after I done stressed over and over to this hoe we are done, she still trying to wig out and check me at the damn mall in public like she don't know who the fuck I am. It took everything in me not to beat her the fuck down. She lucky I got respect for Asha why she approaching a nigga talking about "Really Moe, this what you on? You gone just play me like that with another bitch." Right then and there I could have snapped her neck instantly. For one, you don't disrespect me or embarrass me. Two, you don't disrespect my girl, so this hoe got it coming to her and I'm going to give her what she deserves.

Right after this whole thing Asha ends up in a car accident the next damn day. And for some strange reason, she got it in her head that Lacey was the cause of it. Now the description of the car doesn't match Lacey's car since she has a Lexus. Plus, Lacey ain't the type of chick to do no shit like that, but it's something I will surely look into. I called my nigga Rico to investigate this shit for me. Rico is my main man that do the research when I need someone found. He always finds them no matter how good they hide. Shit a motherfucker can be in protective custody and I bet Rico will still find their ass.

It's been about two weeks since Asha's car accident, and I'm glad she is finally home and safe. So far all we found was the car burned and abandoned in the woods by *Gleason Park*. I was getting a little frustrated because I still haven't dealt with Lacey's ass since

I didn't want to leave Asha's side. Plus, knowing that these motherfuckers are still out there, I had to protect her at all times. You never know what to expect.

Now, here it is almost her graduation and I had plans to take her on a trip to Miami when I meet my connect from Mexico there. It's just a little get away for her to relieve some stress and a pre-graduation gift. I decided to let her cousin come since Weed will be with me handling our business.

I told Autumn to keep it a secret since it was a surprise for her graduation. We were set to leave on Thursday right after her doctor's appointment because she was on weekly check-ups since the accident to make sure the baby was progressing normally. The look on her face was priceless when we made it to the airport and boarded my private jet. To top it off, her cousin and Weed were already on board so they jumped out screaming surprise. We had the whole jet decorated in graduation décor and a congratulations grad cake with sparkling wine and food.

She just sat there and cried saying we shouldn't have and went on and on about not having clothes because she didn't pack. Of course, you know that was part of my surprise as well. See, I owned a mansion out in Miami, and I had already called up my butler to go shopping for her, so she had a whole brand new wardrobe waiting. I also had one of the bedrooms redecorated into a nursery for her son. Yea, when I say I get what I want, I mean I get what I want, and she was gone be my Mrs. by any means. We arrived in Miami and got settled into the home, and all Asha could do was hug and continue to kiss me and say thank you the whole time. Of course she wouldn't come out of the nursery. Her and Autumn steady snapping pictures of it.

I wasn't set to meet my connect till tomorrow so I decided to take the ladies out to one of my clubs I owned and showed them how Miami gets down. Last time I saw Asha in a club was the club I owned back in Gary *The Link Bar* when we first met, so I'm curious to know how she hits this dance floor with a basketball belly. I took them to *Club Play* since there was a concert scheduled tonight. It will give them a chance to have VIP seats and meet the celebrities. The line into Club Play was wrapped around the building and we were almost at capacity already. We walked straight in and the whole club seemed to pause and have all attention on us.

The DJ immediately came over the mic and said, "Okay Ladies and Gents, before I bring out the next artist, let's give a warm welcome to the Big Man of the house, Mr. Monroe King and his guest!!!"

Everyone greeted us and clapped of course. I had Asha on my arm so she was getting them looks from a few broads that I either had or wanted me. After getting seated at the VIP section, the first artist that came out was Yo Gotti. Asha and Autumn headed straight to the dancefloor to dance to "DM":

I see your girl post her BM, so I hit her in her DM

All eyes yeah I see 'em, yeah this your man I hate to be him

(whoop)

It goes down in the DM (it go down) it go down in the DM (it go down, it go... down)

It goes down in the DM (it go down) it go down in the DM (it go

down, it go... down)

All I could do was watch her work. She most definitely wasn't letting her baby bump stop no show. I guess she had to show me she still had it because every move she made she looked at me to make sure I was watching.

Damn, I swear a nigga was getting hard just by watching her dance. I was ready to take her ass into the bathroom or something, and as soon as we were all enjoying ourselves, it takes one dumb ass fuck nigga to fuck shit up. I just so happened to look down and these two drunk motherfuckers want to dance all up on Asha and Autumn like it was sweet. Now, I know good damn well these pussies seen them walk in with us, so why the fuck will they test me I have no clue but they were surely about to learn. Me and Weed made our way to the dancefloor all along the ladies trying to walk away from the dudes and let them know they were cool.

Now what piss me off even more is one nigga had the nerve to grab my bitch by the arm and pull her back to him, and then he grabs her butt. I must have blanked the fuck out, because I was beating the dog shit out of dude. I know for a fact I busted his nose and broke a couple ribs when I stomped him out because you could hear them motherfuckers when they snapped, crackled, and popped.

The only reason I came to was because I heard Asha yelling, "Moe stop! Stop! It's okay. Leave him alone. Let's just dance!!"

I looked at her and she looked so frightened I had to apologize and tell her, "I protect what's mine and what belongs to me, and I refuse to sit here and let you or me be disrespected so if I got to kill a nigga over you, then that's just what the fuck I got to do."

I don't know what it is but it's just something about Asha that makes me feel like I'm her protector. She is just the most precious thing to me and I will die protecting her. This is the first time I have ever felt like this about any female. Yea, I have to admit, she got my nose wide open.

After the little incident, my security came to clear the dudes off the dance floor and throw them out of the building. Yo Gotti was still on the stage during his thing and everyone was still dancing like nothing ever happen. Asha wanted me to stay on the dance floor with her so we started dancing when Yo Gotti got to performing his next hit "Law".

Don't fuck no bitch that's fucking with your dawg, that's law

If you come up don't forget about your dawgs, that's law

I'm a street nigga so its fuck the law

If you broke nigga that should be against the law

I peeped a little shorty I used to fuck with eyeing me down while I was dancing with Asha, so when Yo Gotti exited the stage, I had Weed escort the girls back to the VIP section while I headed to the bathroom. I knew exactly what shorty wanted, and I was down to give it to her, because her head game was bomb. Shorty did some amazing tricks with her tongue piercing that made a nigga feel like he was a cloud nine. After what just went down, I needed that shit right about now.

Just as I expected, she was in the last stall and went straight for a nigga's dick when I walked in. Baby girl was slurping and slobbing all on a nigga's knob. Had a nigga's toes all curled up and shit. Honestly, I didn't think shorty had any tonsils, because she was able to put my balls and my big ass dick in her mouth at one time, and that alone drove me crazy. As soon as I was about to get my rocks off, Weed text saying Asha was headed in my direction DAMN!! I pushed shorty off me and headed out the bathroom before Asha got there, and this little slut runs out the bathroom after me saying, "So you just gone leave me hanging for this pregnant bitch here, and I know this can't be your baby."

Why the fuck did she go and say some shit like that because before I knew it, I backhanded the shit out of shorty. Man can anything else happen tonight?

Chapter 19- Falling

Asha

Two weeks after getting released from the hospital, I was glad to say that me and LJ (Lorenzo Jr.) were doing good. Due to me going into preterm labor, my doctor started me on weekly visits which was cool because we got a good report card every week. I'm due to graduate the following week with honors and earn my ADN. Things were going good, and me and Loco started to get along for the sake of our son. Me and Moe's relationship was moving forward, and I have to say I was truly falling for this man hard. He just seems to amaze me more and more each day.

Moe was the last person I expected to stay by my side the entire time I was in the hospital. I mean, for real though y'all, a man with his status, you would have thought he had business to handle, but instead, he either got someone else to take care of it or he put it aside. He didn't leave that hospital till I left. That alone made me fall head over heels for him. I was truly in love with this man.

Moe had informed me that he was looking into my accident. He said he doubt that it was ol girl Lacey because she didn't have that in her but he was sure to check her whereabouts doing that time to make sure. What Moe didn't know was I had already found out who did it. See while in the hospital I got a text from Cinnamon stating, **"I didn't succeed this time. I will be sure to succeed the next time. I will be the one and only baby mother Loco has."** This was a beef I needed to personally handle alone.

Since I knew it wasn't Lacey, I knew she would be okay and Moe wouldn't harm her. I did not want to give him any suspicion that I was hiding something from him so I let him continue to look hoping he didn't find out it was Cinnamon before I got to her. I just sat back and was contemplating my next move because it was gone have to be my best move against this bitch.

When I got home, Moe had a surprise lined up for me and man what a surprise it was. I was shocked that he was able to get Autumn to keep her mouth closed about the surprise because everyone knows that bitch can't hold water when she gets excited. Anyway, about this surprise though y'all. It was truly amazing. See Moe took me on his own private jet. Yea, that's right, I said his own jet, Now, this jet was luxurious as hell, straight plushed out. Talking about riding in style in the air though. To top it off he had it decorated for me with all types of graduation décor.

Yea, I was cheesing from ear to ear and in tears when I saw this. I felt special as hell and you know this pregnancy got me sensitive as hell too so I was overly excited. We partied a little on the jet on our way to Miami and all, but damn, the real party was as soon as we touched down. I know y'all probably like how the hell am I partying and shit pregnant. I need to sit my hot ass down right, but hey, I had to get it in one last time before I dropped my load. Plus, I deserved it all. Nursing school is stressful than a bitch for real. Not to mention, I haven't been out since I met Moe and don't know one monkey stop no show, so pregnant people deserve to have fun too.

So we arrived in Miami and went to get settled in at Moe's mansion, and when I say mansion, I mean mansion. This was the most beautiful place I have ever seen, and I have seen some big nice houses before but never to this extent. We pulled up to a big ass security gate with guard. The only way you're getting on this property is if you are invited there; it was that secure. It had a wraparound driveway which seemed to be at least two miles long before you made it to the front entrance of the house.

Walking through those big white doors and seeing those white marble floors was breathtaking. The house has a five car garage, with six bedrooms, four bathrooms, a huge kitchen with lots of cabinet space, dining room, and an indoor swimming pool with a hot tub and sauna. He had the basement converted into a theater just like the movies and a separate room that was a studio. It looked like he hired an interior decorator to furnish the house because the décor was immaculate. Now the most important part of the house was yet another one of my surprises.

The master bedroom was huge; it looked like another whole house. I honestly don't know what kind of bed it was because he had it custom made and it was bigger than a California King. But the master bathroom was gorgeous; this bathroom gave me life with the his and her sinks, walk-in rain shower that was also a sauna, and a huge Jacuzzi tub. There are his and her walk-in closets and he had my name engraved on my closet that was already filled with the finest designer clothing and shoes. The master suite was joined with a nursery that was painted blue and white and had LJ on the door.

I was in total awe and speechless. I just sat there and cried like a little bitty baby. All I can say is, "When did you do all this and why?"

He kissed me and said, "Anything for my queen and to see that beautiful smile upon your face." Listening to those words roll off his tongue made me want to christen the bed, bathroom Jacuzzi, and shower right then and there. Of course, we didn't have time because the celebration had just begun.

We all got dressed and prepared to go to another one of his establishments called *Club Play*. This club was packed as shit way before midnight. I'm guessing because of the concert they were hosting but I mean damn Miami was out y'all. Me and Autumn was excited as hell to have front row VIP seats to this concert. We got to see and meet Beyoncé and she sang my song *"Formation"* y'all. Yes, me and Autumn got straight in formation too soon as we heard

Y'all haters corny with that Illuminati mess

Paparazzi, catch my fly and my cocky fresh

I'm so reckless when I rock my Givenchy dress (stylin')

I'm so possessive so I rock his Roc necklaces

I have to admit, Bey did her thang on the stage too and our VIP section was the best seat in the house. Yes, she did that. To make matters worse, my nigga Yo Gotti was there and everyone knows I love me some Gotti. Hell Gotti can get it any day to be honest. Shush y'all don't tell Moe I said that though. But you know me and Autumn hit that dance floor soon as the DJ announced Gotti. We stayed there on the dance floor majority of the night. Autumn said I was going to dance myself into labor when DLOW did the "Do It Like Me Challenge". Yep Moe let us get right up on stage and dance with them. We got down and was right on cue with the

Ooh, oh

Ah, ah

Hey, hey, turn up

Oh, oh

Having a ball this night was truly an understatement. I had the time of my life. Granted we did run into a few complications like Moe damn near beating a dude to death for being drunk and trying to dance with me. HaHaHa this man is a trip; he really wants to protect me and act like there isn't going to be a man in sight that will look at me. I mean, damn. I have to say I'm a bad ass chick and me being pregnant didn't make it no better cause pregnancy looks good

on me.

Anyway we got Weed putting niggas to sleep and shit for

fucking with Autumn. Females talking shit up under their breath

because they feel some type of way about us being with Moe and

Weed, but here goes the kicker. I got bitches trying to fuck my man

and shit in the bathroom while he here with me. Now, you know I

wanted to slap the shit out this little bitch.

And that right there ended my perfect night. Moe knew I was

pissed off and had beef towards him as well. The whole way home I

didn't say shit to him. I guess that motherfucker thought I didn't peep

him and the nasty pussy bitch making eye contact. I knew what the

fuck was up. I went through enough of that bullshit with Loco's ass,

and I be damn if I go through the same shit with Moe. I told Autumn

that I was catching the next flight home and she can either come or

stay her choice.

"Haaaa really though shorty. Stop flexing your ass ain't going no motherfucking where so you can calm the fuck down and cut all that extra shit out."

Autumn and Weed just sat there looking and waiting on me to respond back to Moe and all I can do was roll my eyes and say, "Whatever Autumn. You heard what I said."

So this nigga had the nerve to get in my face and say, "Oh so you think I'm playing with you huh? You heard what the fuck I said. Now, you can take your ass in the house and go upstairs to get ready and take this dick. Now, that's the only place you're going and the only thing you gone do. Now play with it if you want to."

Now that shit right there pissed me off even more. I don't know who the fuck he thought he was so what I did was sit up and got back in his face like I was really doing something.

"I don't know what the fuck you think this is or who the hell you think I am but there's no way I'm gone sit here and let you play me like I ain't shit and gone be cool with it. Hell, I went through enough of that with Loco's ass, and I be damned if I go through it with you, so like I said, I'm leaving and you can call your little slut and fuck her."

"First off, Mrs. Lady, I didn't fuck the bitch. All the little bitch did was suck my dick. Second of all, the only motherfucker I'm putting my dick in is you. Who gives a fuck about a bitch wanting to slob on my balls, as long as that's all I'm giving her. Now again, this my last damn time saying this. We can do this the easy way and you can take your little ass up the stairs willing and get ready to receive this big ass dick, or I can carry your ass up there. Either way it goes, you are going in that room and you getting this dick tonight so make your choice wisely."

After his last statement and that look in his eyes, I knew right then and there this man was not about to play with me so guess what I did? I took my happy go lucky ass right on up the stairs like I was told, but did it with an attitude and slammed the door. The only difference was I went to the bathroom to get in the shower. I still have a point to prove. Hell, he doesn't control me. As I'm running the water for the shower and about to take off my clothes, I hear the song "Promise" by Kid Ink come on

I do tell you what you wanna hear

Hope it don't go in and out of one ear

You the only one that I wanna stare at in the mornin'

Girl cause you one of them

I turn around and see Moe standing there butt ass naked. Umm this man is gorgeous with or without clothes. I instantly felt my juices start running down my legs. He picked me straight up and got to tongue kissing me down; he placed me in the shower with my back up against the wall. He lifted me up and filled my love spot all the way up with his tongue.

That feeling along that he was giving me had my mind going in circles. I felt so vulnerable to his touch. His touch alone overpowered me. Every time this man touched me it felt like shock waves were shooting through my body. As he proceeded to play with my nub and make circles with his tongue, my body began to shake.

He started to pick up the pace and fuck me with his tongue, and I couldn't take that pleasurable feeling anymore. I instantly climaxed feeling his mouth up with my juices while he was steady sucking me dry.

He gently slid me down off the wall and positioned me over his rod. I passionately kissed him as he gently inserted himself into me. Ooh this man felt so good as he proceeded to thrust into me. I grinded my hips to match him. The faster he went, the harder I grinded. I couldn't help but to throw my head back as that painful good feeling that I wanted to last forever filled me up. At that point, I knew right then and there that I became victim to the Mr. Monroe "Moe" King's fan club because there was nothing this man can do to make me leave him. He was like my drug addiction, and I was addicted bad. Rehab couldn't break this addiction.

Chapter 20- Mind Blowing

Lacey

So me and Loco have been getting close these past few months. Granted, I haven't muscled up the courage to open my legs to him yet, but we have been dating for a while. Honestly, I'm a little scared to fuck him because I don't know what to expect. Hell, I only had sex with one nigga and one nigga only, and that's Moe. It did get close the other night when Loco and I went to the movies and we almost got busy in the car. I had to hurry and jump up because his shit felt a little bit too big for my liking through them jeans. Oh Lord what am I going to do with that is all I thought.

I finally overcame my phobia on getting broke off by Locos' anaconda and decided tonight was the night I will let him break my back. I mean let's be honest now y'all. I haven't had sex in months. Me and Moe wasn't on good terms and stopped talking and I spent enough money on some damn *Pure Romance* toys that I needed the real deal. I mean, sure the toys were good and all for the time being but you get tired of getting yourself off by yourself after a while. Anyway, I decided to cook dinner for him and have us chill and watch some Netflix.

Earlier that day, I went and picked out this sexy ass little black Christian Dior spaghetti strapped dress to go along with my black Christian Dior stilettos. I stopped over at Victoria's Secret to get a cute little sexy bra and panty set to match. I already had the roast in the crock pot going. I just needed to prepare the homemade mashed potatoes, corn, and dinner rolls. Yes, a Sista was a beast in the kitchen. After finishing the dinner, I ran me a bubble bath to soak before it was time. It was a good thing that I had my Brazilian done two days prior before I decided to let him go down there geesh.

After bathing, I lotion my vanilla Carmel skin down with my *Sweet Pea* lotion I got from *Bath and Body Works* and topped it off with the body spray to match. I lit the candles on the dinner table, had dimmed the lights, and had Dreezy playing softly in the background

My body, your body

(All over your body, baby)

My body, your body

My body, your body

Loco was due to arrive in another 15 min and my nerves were all over the place. I checked myself in the mirror one last time to make sure my hair and everything was in place and then the doorbell rang. My heart instantly dropped; I have never been this scared and nervous before just to see a dude, so I knew it was really about to go down. I opened the door and greeted my boo, "Hey bae," and pecked him on the lips.

"What's up, Ma. Damn, you looking good," and he smacked me on my ass when I turned to walk away from him. I couldn't help but to giggle because that turned me on.

"I hope you brought your appetite and are ready to eat," I said as I was leading him to the dinner table.

"Shit, for real though, Ma. The way you looking I can skip dinner and go straight to the desert and just eat you all up," he said while licking those sweet juicy lips of his.

I swear the way this man was looking oh so sexy a bitch was ready to pounce on his ass, but I'm lady so I had to keep my composure. All I could do was sit there and smile and have him sit at the table.

"Okay lil momma; I see you. This shit looks good and smell delicious."

"Well, just wait till you taste it, because I'm the truth when it comes to the kitchen."

We both laughed and started to eat. For the remainder of the night, we sat, joked, laughed, and tried to watch Netflix, but the movie that was on was *Love & Basketball*. And baby I tell you when it got to the part with Omar Epps and Sanaa Lathan about to do it for the first time, it seemed like that was the green light for me and Loco.

We were on each other like white on rice tonguing one another down. Mind you I just went to *Victoria's Secret* to purchase this panty and bra set and this fool ripped my panties clean off me. He almost ripped my dress off too, but I got to it before he did and removed it over my head which gave him the perfect time to slip his finger in my vagina. I moaned with so much emotion and threw my head back to take it all in. He passionately kissed me on my neck and moved down to my sweet plump and juicy breast and flicked his tongue across my nipple. I screamed out loud with so much ecstasy from the way this man was making me feel.

I just couldn't control myself while he was finger fucking me and using his tongue to play with my nub. That alone had a bitch mind blown and body got to convulsing like I was having a seizure. I came so hard and so fast you would have thought the sink was overflowing. He looked up at me and smiled; all he can say was,

"Yes baby. Come for daddy. You know you want it," and before I can catch my breath, he put all himself deep down inside of me.

"Uugghh," I said so loudly. That shit was hurting oh so good. I was so stuck I was afraid to move he was so far up in me. I started to claw at his back and he grabbed my hand and held them down and went deeper. I thought he was going to burst out of my stomach. He was that far inside me.

He flipped me over to hit it from the back, "Oooh shit; oooh shit," was all I can say once he was in there. The thrust he was giving me was so long and deep; he grabbed my hair and pulled my head back with one hand and took the other and inserted his finger into my ass. Now I never been the type to do anal, but his finger being inside of my ass and his dick going so far up in me was feeling so good, I was willing to do any and everything for this man.

"Damn baby girl, this pussy feels so good you like this dick huh?"

All I can do is moan and say, "Yes," over and over again.

He pushed me down on the bed and had my ass straight in the air as he licked me from front to back. He literally fucked my ass and pussy with his tongue so good I came multiple times.

"Yea I see you like it like that huh? You want some more of daddy dick?"

I nodded my head yes as he inserted his dick in my ass and I tried to run. He held me down and said, "No, you about to take this dick. You said you wanted it, now you got it, so take this shit like you supposed to." He smacked me on the right ass cheek and was pounding in my ass so hard and so fast all I could do was grip the sheets and scream as tears ran down my face while he continued to blow my mind.

Chapter 21- Message

Loco

So, it's been a few months since Asha's accident but ever since that day things between me and Cinnamon have been chaotic. Any and everything I did she threw Asha up in my face and I was getting tired of the shit. All this bitch fucking did is nag nag nag all day every day. It was so bad instead of us talking like we use to we fucked and we fought, fought and then fucked. I had started to think she picked fights with me just, so I can fuck her.

Damn man I couldn't even be a father to my kids and spend time with them without her having something to say. I fed them, it was I'm doing it wrong. She will say shit like, "What the hell? You too busy thinking about this baby with Asha you can't even feed the twins right." I got so tired of going upside this bitch head on a regular I stop being there that much. You would think this hoe would have got tired of having a busted lip, or black eye, and getting her wig split that she would have kept her mouth shut and showed some respect, but instead she ran her shit even more. I was beginning to think she liked for me to whoop that ass. That it was some type of turn on or something for her. I don't know but the bitch is sick in the head for real.

Just the other night, she said something slick out the mouth and before I knew it I popped that hoe dead in the mouth and the bitch started sucking my dick and licking the blood and shit off her lip. I don't know what type of relationship you call this shit, but hey, like they say, the grass ain't always greener on the other side, and I learned that shit the hard way. Now y'all don't go thinking I'm just some type of woman beater and shit, because it ain't even like that, but trust and believe, I demand my respect. I don't give a fuck if it's from a nigga or a bitch; you gone respect me regardless. Especially if you my woman. You gone learn to stay in a woman's place and watch your mouth when it comes down to talking to me or get the shit slapped outcha. Yea granted when I was with Asha, we fought just as well, but it was on some drunk shit or because she thought I was cheating and she will go upside my head first, and yea nine times out of ten, I was cheating, but we never amounted to no shit like this.

Anyway, I stopped fucking with Cinnamon like that period. I mean literally stopped fucking with her. It wasn't no sex, no sleeping in the same bed, no shit. Granted, we still lived in the same household and all, because I wanted to be around my kids, but technically, I ignored the shit out of her. When I left the house, I stayed gone and didn't come home till I was ready to pass out. I either slept on the couch or on the floor in the twins' room. Hell, I wasn't fucking with this looney bitch.

The fact that Asha was pregnant really had this chick in her feelings, and the way she was acting, I really didn't know what she was capable of, and I didn't trust her. Besides all that, ol girl Lacey I told y'all about earlier, we had started getting close and kicking it lately. So when I wasn't out on the block hustling making my paper and handling business, I was always with Lacey's sexy ass. We were getting closer and closer the more time we spent together. I'm not sure what happened to her dude, and frankly, I can care less. All I knew was she was good as got and was going to fall victim to my dick just like all these other thots round here because I was on a mission to tear that pussy up. As long as I kept playing my cards right, I knew she was bound to give it up.

One night, I got a text from Lacey that said, **Hey Bae I want you to come over here today and I cook for you instead of us going out. Is that okay?"**

Bingo, there it is. I knew she would be giving up them draws sooner or later. I responded back to her letting her know it was cool and the time was set for 6:30 tonight. I took a nap with my daughter at like 3:30 that evening and Cinnamon had my son. By the time I woke up, it was like 5:00 so I hopped in the shower to get ready for the night, and just like that, here this hoe goes starting some shit again. Seriously y'all, I was miserable. You mean to tell me a nigga can't wash his balls after you done seen me sitting here knocked the fuck out. She still hollering who I been fucking that I got to take a shower and shit.

I just shook my head and went and showered; I ended up putting on this Ralph Lauren outfit with some LeBron's' to match. I got my gold chain with the cross hanging on it and my Rolex watch, sprayed some of my Gucci cologne on, and as soon as I'm coming out the bedroom, she posted waiting for me. At this point, I had had enough. if she says anything to me I'mma let her have it, and sure enough, here she goes neck rolling and all.

"So Loco where the fuck you going smelling and looking all good. Let me guess, Asha's house?"

I closed my eyes, took a deep breath, and let her have the truth. "Naw, I ain't going over Asha's house, hell. I wish I was, but I ain't. We don't fuck with each other like that, and I don't know how many times I got to tell you that, but since you want to know, I'm about to go get up in this bitch pussy after I eat what the fuck she cooked for me so I can get the hell away from your shit starting nagging ass. Now excuse me, I got a sexy ass redbone waiting for me."

All she can do was stand there and look stupid. Once what I said actually hit her, she tried to come at me swinging and I grabbed her little ass and pinned her on the couch and told her about herself.

"Look Cinnamon, this ain't what you want girl. I will fuck you up seriously. Now look, I told you from jump street I didn't want to be with you like that, and I wanted to be with Asha, but since I couldn't have Asha anymore and you were pregnant I tried to work things out with you. Now for some strange reason, you acting nuts all day every day. You so fucking busy worried about Asha when you should have been worried about all these other hoes out here that want me. Now last time we got into it, I told you I was done with your simple ass. I'm not fucking you. My dick hasn't been in you in almost a month so who I fuck is none of your concern. Wait no, scratch that. I wouldn't give a flying fuck if I was still fucking you. Hell, if another bitch gone let me smash, then I'm going to smash. You should have known off top I would never be faithful to you. Hell, look at how you got me. I wasn't faithful to the one person who has my heart so what makes you think I would be faithful to a bitch

I can care less about. Hell, the same way you got me is the same way you will lose me, so I suggest you fall the fuck back and kick rocks with all this bullshit."

And just like that, I walked out the door to head to Lacey's house. Once in the car, I text Lacey to let her know I was in route and I will be there in about 15 minutes. I turned on my radio and my song got to playing; it was just what I needed to relax and take my mind off what just happened between me and Cinnamon. I fired up my blunt and bobbed my head to the song *The Hills* by The Weekend:

Your man on the road, he doing promo

You said keep our business on the low-low

I'm just tryna get you out the friend zone

Cause you look even better than the photos

Once I made it over to Lacey's house, I was in a better mood and more relaxed, but damn, when baby girl opened up that door, I must say a nigga got excited as hell. She looked good than a motherfucker. I wanted to skip dinner and eat her ass up right then and there. My dick got hard instantly; shorty had on this tight ass black dress that hugged all her curves, those high heeled shoes made that ass lift up even more and she was bowlegged what made it so bad. Man she had a nigga drooling for real. Hell, I had to pick my mouth up; I think shorty was planning for it to go down tonight. Huh she just doesn't know what she got herself into.

Me and shorty sat down and ate and I must say homegirl can cook. We went in her room and cuddled on the bed to watch *Love & Basketball* on Netflix since it was supposed to be a Netflix chill night. We had already established I was spending the night so cuddling in bed was the perfect spot to be. We had a good time laughing and talking; I was really enjoying her company; she took my mind off of everything. Next thing I know, we were going at it tonguing each other down.

Mind you, I already wanted to attack her fine looking ass at the door, and now that I knew it was about to go down for real, I wasn't giving her the chance to back out. My dick was on swole and ready to burst through my jeans. I be damn if I was going to have blue balls tonight; I ripped those panties off so quickly and started massaging that pussy; all she can do was moan. Baby got so freaking wet I could have gotten a cup to drink her juices. Needless to say I tore that pussy up like it was no tomorrow and it was the last time I was going to get some pussy. Hell, I even broke her virgin ass in. I wasn't playing. That shit was just too damn good to pass up and she was just too damn fine. Right after that, we both fell asleep, naked and cuddled up.

The next morning, we both showered and got dressed since I had some business to handle. I wasn't ready to end our time together so I let her come along. Me and the fellas met up over Nate's crib because we had to make a drop and grab so more work. Nate was trying to get at least three kilos to give to our trap houses in East Chicago. The work out that way was moving a lot quicker than in Gary because of the beef we had with Moe and his crew.

Now see I never really discussed anything to the fellas about Lacey besides the fact that I met this fine ass redbone. That's all they knew; they never seen her till today, and they never knew her name. As soon as we pull up to Nate's crib, he tells me we need to go to the warehouse. Now the warehouse is located over there by 2nd Ave where the train tracks is and behind the old *US Steele Mill*. The only time we go to this warehouse is if we about to body a nigga so trust and believe when I say I was confused I was confused but I followed my peeps right on over there. I figured they must've knew something I didn't know or possible had one of Moe's guys tied up in there and wanted my approval to off his ass.

We get inside the warehouse and Nate pulls me to the side. I tell Lacey to have a seat for a second and I will be right back. This nigga Nate had the nerve to tell me that Lacey is fucking with the enemy and she might be here to get information on me so this nigga Moe can get at me. So, I'm like whoa nigga what the fuck are you talking about. He says, "Fam, ol girl is Moe's bitch my nigga. That ain't just some random ass chick. That's his bitch nigga!" So I look at Lacey and back at Nate like naw man that can't be. My man's pulls out his IPhone and google an event this nigga Moe had at one of his clubs and shit. And what do you know there's a picture just as bright as day with this bitch and this nigga arm and arm all lovey dovey and shit.

I snatched the phone out of Nate's hand and walked over to Lacey and said, "Lacey what the fuck is this shit?" she looked at me like I was crazy, which only pissed me off even more so I yanked her up by her arm and asked her, "Who the fuck is this nigga you with in this pic? Who the hell is he to you?"

All she said was, "Ouch Loco you're hurting me. I don't know what you're talking about. Let go Loco!!"

I grabbed her by her hair and said, "Bitch look at the damn picture. Is this your nigga?"

She took the phone and said, "That's me and Moe, my ex, that I told you about. Why? What is wrong?"

Yep right there was the wrong answer. I instantly wigged out on her ass. I grabbed her by her neck and started choking the shit out of her screaming at her, "Bitch you trying to set me up? This nigga sent you at me huh? What you were supposed to do fuck me and make me fall for you so this nigga can catch me off my square and off me or something?"

I laughed and looked at Nate and them and said this pussy ass nigga really sent a bitch in after me. Ain't this some shit. Lacey just stood there crying and begging, "Please Loco I don't know what you're talking about. Me and Moe don't talk anymore; he played with another female he got pregnant I wouldn't do that to you."

And right then and there, I told that bitch to shut up and put her ass right to sleep with a bullet to the chest.

"Aye yo Nate, y'all clean this bitch up and drop the hoe on that nigga doorstep or something. Leave that pussy ass nigga a message. Damn man that's fucked up. I was really digging shorty's fine ass too, and her pussy was good. I should have fucked one last

time before I offed her ass Damn!!!"

Chapter 22 – NoWhere to Run

Cinnamon

So, since I didn't succeed with getting rid of Asha and that baby like I had planned my hitman D-Bo came up with an idea to just knock her off in a house robbery. That seemed like the perfect idea till I got a call from this nigga the other day stating she was fucking around with Moe the King Pin of the streets. We knew right then and there we were in over our head. There was no way in hell we would be able to touch this girl without facing some repercussions ourselves so we shut down the whole operation. Thing is, I had already text this bitch and informed her it was me that ran her off the road. She never knew a thing about D-Bo and them covering for me or anything. I know dumb me right, but I just knew I was getting my satisfaction.

Well, I was wrong, and now I'm just walking around here with a target on my head. I learned that word on the street is Moe is looking for the person that was driving the car that ran Asha off the road. He put up $25,000 to the person that can hand deliver me to him. I was shitting bricks waiting on them to come pick me up any second because all along Asha knew who did it. I cussed myself out every day for making that dumb ass mistake and texting this bitch.

All I can do is hit myself in my forehead and yell, "Stupid, stupid, Cinnamon!!!" Here it is, I had nowhere to go, nowhere to hide. All my family was here in Indiana, I had no outside relatives in other cities and states. I have two kids that I just can't up and move out the city, and besides with Moe's reputation, he can find you anywhere. What the hell was I going to do now? This whole situation was weighing down on me so heavy I started taking things out on Loco and we were really on bad terms. Because of my careless and selfish ways, I had pushed Loco away from me completely.

Things were so bad that we hardly ever spoke to each other; he stopped sleeping next to me, and we stopped having sex completely. First, that's all we did was fuck and argue; it was like we argued just to have makeup sex. Now, we don't even acknowledge each other's presence. All I wanted was to go back in time and change things and fix what I have done. Being so spiteful and deceitful has gotten me nowhere and caused nothing but pain and hurt. I was in love with a man who wasn't in love with me, did everything up under the sun to get this man, yet I turn out to be the cause of him walking away from me for good from trying to kill the man that I love baby and the mother. Not to mention I was a mother myself to two beautiful twins that I probably won't see grow up because of my selfish ways.

I thought about coming clean with Loco and telling him everything I did since he chooses to be so bluntly honest and shit with me lately. This nigga was so honest he had the nerve to tell me he was going out with a chick and he was getting him some pussy. Come to think about it I haven't seen or heard from this nigga since, so I'm guessing he all booed up with her since he didn't come home last night and haven't bothered to check up on the twins. Let me try some shit like that and tell him some shit like that, I will have an extra knot upside my head. Oh well I guess it is what it is. Like he said, I can't expect nothing no different when I got him the same way.

I decided to call up my sister and let her know that I was giving her the combination to the safe that is in the back of my closet. I informed her that if there was anything to ever happen to me, the directions on how to go about things will be in my will and it also states who the twins should go to. Of course, this got my sister worried but I had to play it off and just tell her I'm thinking like a mom you know tomorrow is never promised, so I want to make sure my kids are good and safe just in case. She didn't stress to me anymore or try and dig out more information from me. She just said okay and told me she loved me. After disconnecting the call, I sat on the couch and rolled me up a big fat blunt.

I was all set and prepared to go take a relaxing bubble bath to clear my head. I had my blunt rolled, IPod ready to go, Moscato on ice, and had a nice hot bubble bath waiting for me. Before getting in the tub, I decided to spend some time with the twins and get them dressed. I gave them both a bath and fed them, put them on some matching outfits, and played with them for a while. In the midst of all that, they fell asleep. Since it was nice out, I decided on taking them to the park once I got out the tub.

Even though they were too young to really play on anything I wanted to get as much time in with them as I could because I didn't know what the future held for me. I had started to realize that it was really true what they say. Don't no baby keep no man. Granted, I had no intentions on having kids but once I got pregnant I thought it was an added bonus to get Loco. Yet all in all till this day he still doing him. I was so depressed and mind all out of whack that I turned the IPod on and Future ft. The Weekend song was on *Low:*

I just took some molly, what else? (Hey)

Got some bitch from Follies with us ('scuse me, 'scuse me)

She gonna fuck the squad, what else?

I'm a fuck her broads, what else?

I lit my blunt, submerged myself in the water, held my head back, took a sip of my Moscato, grabbed my Full Bloom toy from

Pure Romance and went to work letting everything flow out my mind.

Chapter 23- What Goes Around Comes Around

Moe

After leaving Miami and making it back to Gary, Asha was set to walk across the stage. Of course, you know I had to have my baby go out in style with a stretched out all-white Bentley Limo that matched her all-white suit. Of course them hoes was straight jealous of my bae when she pulled up looking flawless as ever. She had all of her family and friends there to support her and I even rented out the *Marquette Park Pavilion* to throw an all-out celebration for all her graduating class. I was finally able to meet her family and she met mines since I invited a few of them as well.

That was months ago and boy I tell you if her, Autumn, and my sister Liz don't get on my nerves. I don't know what I'm going to do. A nigga can't even bust a nut without one of them calling and putting the other on three-way. Since they met, they done got close as hell. With that being said, of course my family took Asha in and was willing to accept the baby when he got here as part of the family knowing it wasn't my child. That was a good feeling and gave me more clarification on making her my Mrs. I planned on proposing to her this weekend at an event we have coming up at one of our clubs.

So once the time came for the event to take place, I had everything set and in place. I had got Jagged Edge lined up to make an appearance and perform at the club because this is her favorite throwback group of all time. I made sure her family and mines were present and set to walk out once they started to sing *Promise:*

> Nothing is promised to me and you
>
> So why will we let this thing go
>
> Baby I promise that I'll stay true
>
> Don't let nobody say it ain't so

Right on cue, they came out when me and her hit the dance floor. Of course they were going to let her know it was dedicated to her from me. Once she saw her family and friends plus mines, she started crying and smiling from ear to ear. Once they finished singing *Promise,* Jagged Edge themselves escorted her to the VIP section with everyone lined up watching, and they started to sing *Let's Get Married:*

See first of all

I know these so-called playas wouldn't tell you this

But I'ma be real and say what's on my heart

Let's take this chance and make this love feel relevant

She was looking so lost and looking around at everyone waiting on someone to give her some kind of hint to what was going on. I came up the middle of the aisle with the ring in my hand. I got down on one knee and proposed. I got everything on video since the whole event was getting videotaped because this girl screamed from the top of her lungs and said yes. Right then and there I was the happiest man on earth.

Yea I bet y'all like, this corny ass nigga, but hey, thugs need love too, and I wanted this to be special not only for her, but for me too. And to show and prove to her that I mean this. I said earlier that if I found the right one I will settle down and leave all this bullshit alone. As soon as I was reminiscing on our engagement and thinking about getting out the streets, this nigga Weed calls with some bullshit. He tells me that Lacey's body was found and she was shot in the chest and her body was dumped in the front of my old crib. Damn man, these niggas just not gone learn and let me be. Every time I try to leave that life, a bitch ass nigga sucks me right back into where I have to go right back and prove my point.

We already knew off top who did the shit. Plus, I was told she was already fucking around with the nigga. Me and Asha went to the scene of the crime and the coroner was just now picking her body up and loading her in the truck. I didn't even get a chance to see her but it was a good thing my crew was there and saw her, so they were able to update me on the condition of her body. Lacey's mother and father was present on the scene and it hurt me to my soul to hear her mother screaming and yelling like that. I walked over to her parents to give them my condolences and her mother slapped the shit out of me and said, "It's all your fault! You did this. This is because of you."

Her father grabbed her and took her to the car; he came back and apologized to me and said, "I know you had nothing to do with it; I'm aware that you and Lacey was not together." He asked me to please catch the motherfuckers that did this to his daughter before the police do and make them pay. I told him that I was already on it and not to worry about funeral expenses that it was on me. Asha just stood there looking; I looked at her and gave her the reassurance that I had nothing to do with it.

She looked up at me and smiled and said, "I know, and I know you know who did but Moe please don't do this. I'm carrying this man's child and his family is a part of my son's family."

I couldn't promise Asha anything so I just walked away from her and had Weed take her home. Me and the rest of the fellas stayed there until the police was all done with collecting evidence and questioning everyone. I was so hot and heated and ready to go find this motherfucker I didn't know what to do but pace back and forth. It was fucked up and I knew he did it to send a message because Lacey didn't even know about the house they dumped her body at. These lil niggas really just dumped her like she wasn't shit. Word on the street was the nigga did it when he found out Lacey was my girl, so he thought I sent her in after him.

Fucked up thing is Lacey was no longer my girl and she didn't know shit about him or the beef we had. He never knew me and Asha was in a full blown relationship and due to get married. He thought she cut me off when he told her I was only fucking with her to get close to him. Now this nigga done killed Lacey for nothing and I'm trying my hardest to respect Asha's wishes by not taking her sons' family from him, but the way I feel right now everyone in his family got to go from his mother, sister, brother, friend, cousin, and any other fucking kids he got outside the one Asha carrying. It was about to be a bloodbath in the streets of Gary, IN and I wasn't prepared to back down till his whole operation and crew was taken down.

We sat back and came up with our game plan; the plans were to link up tonight and kill everyone that had something to do with Lacey's murder. I made the exception to let Loco live up until Asha had the baby. After that, this nigga was gone suffer. We went our separate ways to get ready for the night. By the time I made it home, Asha was just now getting out the shower. She looked at me like she was trying to read my mind and figure out what I was thinking.

At that point the only thing that was going through my head was putting my dick inside her, because looking at her standing there with water dripping off her body and nothing on but a towel just woke my mans all the way up. I was licking my lips just thinking about sexing her up and said to her, "Damn, Ma. You might as well drop that towel right now cause I'm about to sex you up." She dropped the towel and laid back on the bed spreading her legs so I can get a full view. She licked her index finger and started to play with herself. I stood there watching, stroking my dick as it got harder and harder from the sounds of her moans. She looked at me and picked up her pace as she had one finger flicking her clit and the other finger she moved rapidly in and out of her pussy.

I went to put my tongue inside her sweet pretty pink pussy and she arched her back, grabbed my head, and pulled me in further. She moved her hips in a circular motion to match the speed of my tongue. As I eased up on top of her to insert myself in her I gave her a long ass tongue kiss. I pushed into her filling her love spot with all of me and she cried out loud. As I started to speed up, and she started to fuck me back, all of a sudden we felt a big ass gush of wet shit on us.

"Damn bae, I know you didn't just come that much?"

I said to her with concern and she had a scared look on her face like something just wasn't right and then she said, "Moe, my water just broke."

Chapter 24 – LJ

Asha

Being addicted to this man didn't serve me no good at all. I just couldn't stay off the dick to save my life and now this is what the fuck I get trying to fuck knowing I had no business fucking at nine months pregnant.

"Oh shit, awe shit!" I yelled as we were on our way to the hospital and all I think about was being addicted to Moe and his dick and how it just broke my water and made me go into labor. I tried to focus and breathe every time a contraction came, but that shit was not working at all. I was screaming and cussing Moe's ass out because to me technically it was all his fault and he the one that broke my damn water. Who the fuck water breaks in the middle of sex? Like where they do that at? This some straight bullshit. On top of that I still didn't get a chance to nut.

"Awe shit, Moe. Hurry the fuck up!!!" I was screaming from the top of my lungs and Moe was flying to the hospital. I was able to call Autumn, Loco, and my family in between the contractions.

Moe had agreed to give me this day and let it be no drama while I'm having the baby. He said he will even leave and let Loco have his shine and he will come back later. In the meantime, he will keep calling to check in on me. I couldn't help but to respect him for that and it meant so much to me that he did that on the count of me and my son with me knowing damn well he wanted to body Loco's ass. I honestly couldn't blame him.

We made it to the hospital at like 3 pm and they took me straight up *to Labor and Delivery*. Ten minutes later, Autumn comes busting through the door giving Moe the okay to leave since Loco would be there soon. The nurse checked my cervix and I was already dilated to 5 cm and my contractions were three minutes apart. They were kicking my ass.

"OOOHHH SHIT! I want an epidural and I want one now. I can't do this shit!!!" I said while having a contraction. I was literally ready to rip the bed rails out the bed.

Now fuck this shit, I know I'm a tough ass bitch but these contractions weren't no hoe, and they had me bitching up really quick. I was not about this life at all. I was begging and pleading for God to show and give me mercy if he only took the pain away. Loco walked in right in the middle of a contraction and I cut him a new asshole. He was all kinds of hoes and bitches. I blamed him and told him it was his fought that he did it to me. Hell, I even threw something at him and I can't even tell you what it was but whatever it was it surely connected and smacked him dead in the face.

Autumn looked and said, "Awe hell naw, bitch fuck that; I ain't never having no damn kids if I'm going to be acting like this shit."

The doctor came in and said, "So I hear you want an epidural. Is that correct?" All I can do was nod my head because another contraction was coming. She said, "Asha I'm going to need to check your cervix again first before administering the epidural because your contractions are coming fast and strong." She checked my cervix and discovered that I was already nine and a half centimeters dilated and it was time for me to push. Loco grabbed one leg and Autumn had the other as I began to push.

LJ was born at 5 pm in the evening weighing 6 pounds, 6 ounces and 20 ½ inches. He was so handsome with a head full of hair and white as day. He came out screaming and peed all on Loco as soon as he cut the umbilical cord. I couldn't help but laugh and cry at the same time. I was so happy to meet my son. Autumn snapped pictures and sent them to Moe's phone. She has been updating him with every detail of LJ's birth since he left.

Holding my baby in my arms, I felt my life was complete. I had a beautiful healthy baby boy, a man that worshiped the ground that I walked on, and I graduated college with an ADN degree. After all the hurt and pain that I had experienced and been through, I never imagined it to turn out for the best. Not to mention, I have a wonderful, loving, supportive, family and friends. On that note, everyone was present to welcome LJ into the world.

Chapter 25 – Busted

Loco

After leaving the hospital when Asha had the baby, I was arrested on drug charges and they sent my black ass straight to the feds. I found out that my niggas Nate and Tone were murdered in a drive-by; the only person that survived was my lil man Ricky and he was in critical condition. The Feds had confiscated 20 kilos of dope that we copped and since the crib was in my name, everything would fall on me.

I was thankful that I was able to see my son come into the world; I also spent some time with the twins before all this shit popped off. The only other thing I can think about was since my life is basically gone, I should have dropped this nut load off in Cinnamon's ass before heading to the damn hospital; Fuck!!

I wasn't set to go in front of the judge for another two weeks, but I knew that with the case they had on me and the evidence I probably wouldn't get a bond, and if I did, that shit was gone be high as hell. What I couldn't figure out was how in the hell they know so much about me and my crew. Did they have someone watching us or was there a snitch in the crew I don't know? The only thing I can come up with is that nigga Moe set me up for killing his bitch. I mean, who else will do this shit, cause he the only enemy I got. The killing part is I don't understand why he didn't collect the money and the work. To top it all off, they were even trying to get me for Lacey's murder. They said they got evidence of that too.

Now the only people who knew about that was Nate and Tone and them niggas dead and we made sure there was nothing left behind. Hell this ain't the first time we done bodied someone and the shit was never traced back to us. I just couldn't understand and figure out how they got all this shit. I called my sister Netta up to see what she had heard and she informed me that they keeping everything hush hush and will only give her my charges. She said that Cinnamon was a wreck so she was bringing her and the twins over to her house to stay for a while. She let me know that my lawyer was already on the case, and I told her to make sure she gives that safety deposit information to Asha and Cinnamon to help take care of my kids.

See the FEDs got me for everything but I was smart. I got a safety deposit box in my sister's name a while ago to help save up money in a time like this, so I would never be without, and as of now, I needed that money to support my kids. I was due to see my kids and baby mommas tomorrow so I could explain the deposit box then. I told my sister to let me know if she will also be here to visit. And just like that, we ended the call and I slept my time away. Hell, that's all you can do when you're in the joint.

Asha

After getting released from the hospital, I felt a little depressed that Loco was going to miss out on his son, but I have to say I would prefer to have him there than dead. I knew Moe wasn't going to stop until he put Loco in the dirt regardless of the fact that he was my baby's father. He respected me enough to let him see his son being born and that was the only pass that Moe was going to give him. I saw that shit just as clear as day when I looked into his eyes and pleaded with him to leave it alone. I knew Moe was the cause of Nate and Tone's murder, even though he never admitted it to me, and we never talked about it, but after Lacey, it was bound to happen. Moe ended up going back to Miami to handle some business, so Autumn came to stay with me to help me with LJ. Being a new mom was such a blessing to me and I have to say with LJ only being a week old, he was spoiled rotten already. Netta had called me to make sure I was going to be present with LJ for Loco's visit since he had something for us and to remind me that

Cinnamon was going to be there too, so I needed to be on my best behavior. I just laughed at the sound of that. I haven't seen or heard from Cinnamon since she sent me that text after the accident so seeing her face to face was going to be real interesting. Especially since she knows I know what she did.

Since the Fed joint was three and a half hours away from Gary, I had Autumn drive me so I can rest in between dealing with LJ on a car ride that long. I refused to ride with Netta and Cinnamon for obvious reasons. We arrived in Terre Haute five minutes before we were due to be there and I felt violated. I wasn't able to bring in the car seat or baby bag so I settled for one pamper and a bottle. They wanted to search my baby pamper, ran the scanner over his bottle since I didn't bring in the diaper bag and car seat, and on top of that, I had to take off my socks and shoes on that dirty, nasty floor. Ugh, is all I can say.

Netta and Cinnamon arrived right after I got checked in and Cinnamon looked so spooked to see me. I just laughed and headed over to give Netta a hug and let her see LJ. I also wanted Cinnamon to see him and introduce him to his big brother and sister. Plus, let this bitch know she ain't stop shit. I walked up to Cinnamon and laughed at her. She just stood there and looked at me. I said to her, "Baby girl, you ain't do shit. My son is alive and well and as healthy as he can be, but getting REVENGE on you… now that tastes so much better than doing anything to you, know why? Because you tried your hardest to break me, take this man away from me, and keep him from me. All you did was break my heart right along with him and revenge of a broken heart is the sweetest revenge of them all because now don't neither one of us have him," and I walked away just as simple as that.

All Cinnamon did was stand there looking dumb; the correctional officer called my name to go back. We were only allowed to go one at a time. Seeing Loco behind that glass wall brought back so many memories of him going to jail back in the day from us fighting or him being a hot boy. It made me feel some type of way. Loco admired his son through the glass and explained to me what was in the deposit box then out of nowhere he said, "What the fuck is that shit?"

I looked up at him and asked him "What?"

He pointed to my ring, and I said, "Oh, I'm engaged to Moe."

I could instantly see the rage form in his eyes like he wanted to come through that glass on me and he probably would if he could.

He said in a calm voice, "So you mean to tell me after all this, you really about to marry this nigga and have my son around this nigga? What the fuck is you thinking Asha James? Damn this nigga did set me up."

Right then and there was my cue to bust his bubble so I had to tell him.

"Okay Loco, for one, you so damn naïve that you can't even see shit when it's right in front of your face, so let me make this clear. You hurt me deep down in my soul to where I thought it was never a way for me to come back. You took everything I thought I had and cherished about love away. I didn't even feel like I'm capable of loving someone or for that matter I didn't feel like anyone could love me because I spent all this time with you and you didn't love me enough to respect me.

Hell, you had kids on me when we were supposed to be each other's first everything and start our family together. You broke me, and you broke my heart so no Moe never set you up, I did. I set you up the first time, and I set you up this time. I gave them all the proof they needed to build a case on you and proof of Lacey's murder too. To top it off, Lacey was innocent. She was never trying to set you up. She didn't know anything about you and Moe's beef. You killed an innocent woman. I told you once, and I meant every single word. If I wasn't going to be with you and couldn't have you then no other bitch was gone live a happy life with you. Yea, it was me; it was all me. Moe didn't have shit to do with it. I took over your little empire and gave it to him. I let him have it all, and by the way, it's Mrs. Asha King to you as in Mrs. Monroe "Moe" King. I'm already married to him. Revenge is a bitch huh!!!"

To Be Continued

Royal-Loyalty Publications is currently accepting submissions. Please send the first 3 chapters of your manuscript, synopsis, and contact information to

Royal.loyaltypub@gmail.com

Please allow at least one week for response.

Check Out Other Books Published By Royal-Loyalty Publications

You Used To Love Me: A Youngstown Hood Affair

Big Sister Secrets: If Someone Would Have Told Me

Dreams Of History: An Untold Story Of History